"Kay," she said. "You *are* dumb. Ain't been any *real* thing on earth for centuries. You think our big skulls invented all this marvel stuff for fun? You realize what *one* Sensy booth costs to build? Forty-eight." She flicked ash angrily and fixed him with those green-lidded eyes. "Million. Four eight. Million. That's what. You can see it all here. Everything that's ever been on good old Mother Earth. All the old battles, all the sights. Pop told you he was Pyramids. Didn't you hear him? You can do it all, Grommy. *Fight* the battles, *thirst* in the Sahara, *sleep* with Merrilyroe, *eat* a shark, *be* eaten by a shark. You can eat a thousand meals and never take on a calo. You want to be drunk and not be hung over? Milk a cow? Fall into a volcano? You can *do* it here, *feel* it, *see* it. The whole thing, Grommy, and you want the *real* thing?"

She was very offended. . . .

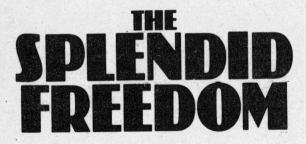

THE SPLENDID FREEDOM

THE SPLENDID FREEDOM

ARSEN DARNAY

SF
ace books

A Division of Charter Communications Inc.
A GROSSET & DUNLAP COMPANY
51 Madison Avenue
New York, New York 10010

THE SPLENDID FREEDOM

Copyright © 1980 by Arsen Darnay

An ACE Book

First Ace printing: December 1980
Published simultaneously in Canada

2 4 6 8 0 9 7 5 3 1
Manufactured in the United States of America

TABLE OF CONTENTS

THE SPLENDID FREEDOM

I

ON HIS twenty-fifth birthday, Grom Gravok left Vizillo to go on his Maturity Trip. A delegation of elders saw him off, mostly younger men; but his father and uncles were also in the group, and so were his mother, two sisters, and Marushka, his bride-to-be. The men were misty-eyed and choked up at departure time. The women cried. Marushka cried most of all. Grom was off to the Splendid Freedom. Would he come back to her? Grom felt a catch of sadness in his throat as he embraced them all, Marushka last. Her face was salty, her lips soft, and her breath sweet. He tore himself away and ran to the mouth of the tunnel that fed the TC Liner *Malinov*. Before he ducked into the tube, he turned and waved once more. On his shoulder hung a red bag labelled Time Collapse Intragalactica.

The night before the entire *gorushka* had gathered to celebrate his coming of age. Three hundred souls, not counting children, filled the

3

basement of Miriam Church on 38th Level. The
tables groaned with eighty-five species of fish.
Wine and *cicillo* flowed. The flat, the deep-
bellied, and the triangulated *balakaikos* resounded with the tremolo. By midnight the men
formed circles and danced the squat-kick *esar-
dasnok*, slowly at first, hands on hips; then faster
and faster; the watchers clapped their hands and
cried "Hay! . . . Hay! . . . Hay!" with every
kick. Faces grew red, then purple. Total strangers
came up to Grom and kissed him with tears in
their eyes. "We'll miss you on the heights," they
said. "Remember us in the Splendid Freedom."
"The mountains," they said; "the prairies blowing in the wind. The solid land." Under the tables
and in corners little children slept with rosy
cheeks. The *gorushka* celebrated until dawn.

He crossed fifty parsecs in three weeks. Then
Malinov broke from Time into Present off the
moon. They landed within hours. Grom took a
number for the shuttle and checked into El-Tuna,
the tourist class lunar transit hotel. His room was
two meta wide and four meta long. One end had a
door, the other a curved space-glass window. It
looked out over the bright gray solidity of craters.
On the third day earth rose over the stark horizon,
a blue-gray spherical magnificence, its face
obscured by a tattered veil of clouds.

Every twenty minutes El-tuna shook from its
foundations up as the catapault discharged
another ship toward the earth. The shuttle never
rested; seventy-two shots a day, without interruption, a thousand souls a shot for the cheap gravity
trip to the Mother planet. Despite frequent depar-
tures, Grom waited a week to make the final leg of

the journey. The station teemed with humanity.

He spent his time in surface exploration. El-tuna rented spacesuits for the purpose and sold maps with excursion hikes marked in a dotted red line. The space port facilities put him off. Luna station never slept. It had a worn, soiled, grimy look. In the eating places the grilles never cooled; the coffee pots forever bubbled; the plastic booths had an oily feel. He didn't dare go to the shows, even if they had been cheap. The Discipline forbade such frivolities, and the Splendid Freedom did not begin until his feet touched terran soil.

He liked the vast, solid emptyness of the moon. He took to the space-suit in no time at all. It was clumsier by far than the grav-suits he was so used to. The principles of motion were the same. In minutes he could run off the horizon and leave Luna station behind. Then he'd stop and stare at the solidity of rock dust. Sometimes he fancied he saw the surface move like a wave. Sometimes a crater lip threatened to spill over like surf. For a man from a water planet, the lunar surface wouldn't hold still, not unless he concentrated on it.

On the sixth day the red light on the intercom was on. A recorded voice gave his departure time the following day.

Splendid Freedom, here I come.

GROM GRAVOK was a structure guard. His twenty-fourth year was the last year of his apprenticeship. His training had begun at age five. When he returned—if he returned—he'd be a journeyman. He wasn't sure at all that he'd return. Some men stayed. Some men left Luna for other places after their Maturity Trip. Grom had seen recruiting booths in the lobby of El-tuna. Structure men were in demand all over Milky Way. Not everywhere was the Discipline strict. He'd even heard of men who worked alone. How, he didn't know. But then the elders didn't tell all, by any means. The foreign pay was very good if you could believe the posters.

A structure guard worked on structures. He built them, he repaired them, and took them apart. Above all, he listened to them; he listened to them even when he had nothing else to do.

The job called for men who had no fear of heights. A good-sized structure on Vizillo reached two mils into the sky. The topmost levels basked in sunshine most of the time, above the clouds. The rich lived there. The lower stories were nearly always under a leaden sky. Vizillo was a water planet. It had virtually no land at all, and those few tatters carried structures. Vizillo circled near the sun and solar heat boiled the southern ocean up to the sky, and the winds drove the water north. The land was in the north. In the equatorial zone ship-cities floated lazily around the globe. The floaters of the South! They knew how to live. Grom didn't know a single structure man who didn't swear he'd retire on a floater. But none ever did. It hurt to leave the structures or the *gorushka*, especially in old age.

A guard lived by the Discipline. They told you from the time you were knee-high: without the Discipline you can't survive in the job. Whether on the outside of a structure, floating free above the ocean—whose ceaseless motion froze into lizzard-skin stillness from great height—or in the deep, dark internal chasms where the gravitron vibes hummed undamped, a man had to listen with a psychic ear. Everyone heard the gross vibrations. Only guards "heard" the subtle tones of grav. It wasn't a hearing in the ordinary sense. It was a knowing. You listened for the "little ones," the "lisping." When the lisping stopped, gravitron failed threatened. If left unheeded, it could lead to structure collapse.

A structure held at least five million people. Grom had heard of structures that held three times that many, but Vizillo had no "giants." Structure guards were much revered. When a guard entered a bar, he drank on the house. Guards had to cultivate humility. Pride made you deaf to the "little ones."

He began service in a grav-suit made for a child. Loose straps tied him to his father like twin umbillical cords. He overcame his terror in a week. A few days later he'd learned to stay upright. He held tools for his father. By age twelve he heard the lisping. The gorushka council tested him with a little black box. Sometimes it lisped, sometimes it just hummed. He passed the test, and there was a celebration.

Discipline flowed from the gorushka. Vizillo was an Anglo world, but all the guards were Slaviros. Grom spoke both languages well. The Anglos called gorushkas "tribes," and they were that; but they were more than that. As the gravdrums in the structure generated gravitron, so the gorushka generated bal. Bal was that subtle unity, that sense of hearing, that ear for lisping. It came from obedience, humility, and brotherhood. What the gorushka demanded of its members was de-

fenseless openness. Without it a man went deaf.
He couldn't hear his own suit fail. He plunged
into the depths.

Twice in his life a guard sailed off into the
Splendid Freedom—at twenty-five, at fifty-five.
Away from the tribe, stripped of the rules, a man
could taste life as it was, unconstrained. He could
test his lust for individualized existence, alone,
free. At twenty-five they went to earth at the
gorushka's expense. To earth, for earth was the
supreme place of freedom. To earth, because earth
had mountains, prairies, deserts. Land, land. And
there civilization had created the ultimate in
human choice. There a man could tray everything. "Splendid freedom," the elders all said.
"Oh, how magnificent is earth! You haven't lived
until you've seen Terra. It's the beginning, Grom,
and it's the end. Vizillo . . . why, it's a backwa-
ter."

The trip cost a hundred and eighty thousand
dulls, most of that for the Time Collapse
journey—a staggering sum, a great gamble for the
tribe. The *gorushka* worked a year to pay off the
loan. Each man gave a tenth of his share. If the
man didn't return, the sum was lost. If two or three
went, the year was lean. Lean years, however,
were part of the Discipline. But so was the Maturity Trip. Without it no man could become an elder.

ALL THIS went through Grom's head as the shuttle
ship, lobbed into space by the catapault, began its
noiseless journey down—or was it up?—to earth.
UP and then down. It was a long trip. The
gorushka had sent him tourist class.

"They owe it to me," Grom thought. He wasn't there yet, but the Splendid Freedom touched his face lightly, like an awakening breeze. He felt a bit defiant. He stretched inner muscles. "They owe it to me, and I owe nothing in return. I've worked on the structures twenty years. I've listened to the song of gravitron. I've slaved sometimes twenty, thirty, fifty hours on the drums without sleep. Many a time, I've floated in the darkness, I've floated in the light, right side up, wrong side around, above the clouds, below them. Once we took a section out in the middle of a storm. The lightning flashed all around us. I think I've had enough of that life. Who wants to float another twenty years before he can escape again? Heeey, freedom. Hey, hey! Brothers and sisters, see this guard *fly*!"

Then he turned once more to his much handled folder, prepared for him by the travel agency. In the upper right hand corner they'd printed his name in gold letters: Grom Gravok. He liked that. He'd never had anything that was quite his own, other than clothes.

He opened the folder and read at random: ". . . entrusted to the care of an experienced Terran family, knowledgeable about the planet's resources, sensitive to your needs, a guide ever on hand . . . or not. *Cozy Pak* gives you the maximum flexibility to structure your trip your way."

He closed the folder. He knew the words by heart. "Structure your trip . . ." Structures kept intruding. Thank the Cosmos they had no structures on earth.

The ship plunged into the ocean at night. It

became a submarine and made for the Northanglo
continent. He was asleep when they docked. An
attendant shook him awake. Sir, sir.

Welcome to Earth, the Planet of Opportunity.
The local time is three a.m., oh-three-hundred for
you lucky Space Marines.

They stumbled down the aisles, a little groggy.
The attendants stood by the exits. They smiled
and said good morning over and over again.

Grom found himself in an enormous hall:
shaped concrete walls, tiled floors, and an echoing of sounds. The letters of the alphabet were
hung on long rods from the ceiling against one
side. They flashed on and off. Many voices, all
different, called mechanically. "All B's step
near." "All F's step near." He followed the sultry
contralto urging the G's. He stopped at a booth
beneath the letter. Near the booth on a bench sat
young men and women. He showed his passport
to the girl in the booth. The girl turned to the
bench. "Gravok," she called. "Anybody here for
Gravok?"

A young woman in slacks and a black silk
blouse stirred and put out a cigarette. She blew
smoke from painted lips and came to him. She
had black, curly hair, green earrings shaped like
half moons, green-tinted eyelids, and long red
nails. She had a strong fragrance.

"Grom Gravok?" she asked. "Cozy Pak Plan?
Hi. I'm the daughter of the house. My name's
Ebullia, but call me Billy. Say, your name isn't
really Grom, is it? Cluny name. Makes me think of
a guy burping. You know, sort of under his
breath."

"Beg your pardon?"

"Oh, never mind. Grom-sock. Pleased to meet you. Let's get out of here and get some sleep. You sure picked a time."

"My luggage . . ."

"Never mind that. It'll come by vaccutube. We're all set for tourists around here, Grommy. Say, let me call you Grommy, kay?"

And she led the way out.

Here it was, the Splendid Freedom. Three in the morning, the city still hummed with life and machinery. It was not unlike a structure, seen from the inside, but there was no gravitron song here. Nothing hung in the sky. All rested on rock, vast, solid, endless continents of rock.

They caught a cab. "Let's splurge," Billy'd said. The cab roared through a tunnel.

"Let me see your folder, Grommy. We just got the fax on you last night, no paper work." After a moment's examination—she held up the folder to see by the light of neons spaced at intervals along the tunnel wall—she gave it back to him. "Shouldn't have splurged," she stated. "My, Grommy, you're cutting it tight. This is earth. Grom-kid. Say, you're not one of those structure guards, are you?" And when he nodded: "Boy, will Pop be happy. Zoowishy, Zoo-zoowishy."

He awoke late the next morning in a tiny cubicle. He turned on the light and looked about. His baggage had arrived while he'd slept. The two bags stood next to the narrow cot, beside the red shoulder bag with white letters that said Time Collapse Intragalactica. He saw his jump suit draped over what now turned out to be an old washing machine. He hadn't noticed that the night before. Next to it stood a stand with old clothing shrouded in plastic. He got up and pulled up the shade over the little window. But outside it was as dark now as it had been when he'd gone to bed. He checked his watch. It was ten in the morning—ten-hundred, you lucky Space Marines. He had expected to see land, trees. Those flying creatures that chirped should be about. The blowing grass of the prairie. Or something like that.

At the door he hesitated, hearing conversation and an unaccustomed tone. The bath was to his left. "Sand box," Billy had called it. He meant to ask her why. The voices came from the right. One of them was Billy's. He listened with the door handle in his hand.

"Bully. Bully. Really bully! Fifty thou. Forty-nine five, to be exact. I say that's bully. That's supposed to cover overhead? An A-14 Cozy Pak. Y'ever hear of such a thing? They're not supposed to sell those any more, facryn! I'll ring his neck, I will."

By the sound that followed, a fist rattled china and silver on a table.

"It's not *his* fault, Pops. He doesn't know from nothing."

"I don't mean *him*. Peter, that rat. Wait till I get hold of little Pete. Goddam, Billy, three weeks on fifty thou. That's not a lot of activities. What're we going to do with him? Jeez, bird, it's nothing. Peter radded us but good."

"You asked him to send us something, anything. I heard you on the visi."

Silence.

"Fifty thou!" The voice was incredulous but resigned. For a moment no sound penetrated two

doors and a hallway. Grom smelled fried food.
"Structure guards!" the voice said, in an intona-
tion that didn't signify approval.

Grom had heard enough to be puzzled and disturbed. Fifty thousand dulls was a fortune on Vizillo.

He opened the door and went to the bath, the
shoulder bag in his hand.

When he emerged a door opened, and Billy said
Hi and asked him to meet Pop. Pop wore an un-
dershirt. He was bald with a crown of hair above
the ears. He smiled at Grom painfully past soiled
plates that had held fried bird eggs. Grom recognized the sight and smell from the El-tuna
eateries. Pop didn't rise. He dabbed ashes from a
dead cigar.

"Hya, stranger. I'm the father of the house. Just
call me Pop, cozy like. Ready for your first joy trip,
are you? Billy!" he called, as a master calls a
servant, "breakfast for the young gentleman. Sit
down . . . eh . . . Mr. Grom . . . eh, Gravok."
Pop had Grom's folder to his left and read the
name on the cover. "Well, how d'you like it so far?
Billy! Continental breakfast, remember? Mr.
Grom . . . Gravok is on A-14. A-14, Mr. Grom."
He nodded, as if in approval. "Healthy and frugal.
Frugality. Very important." He smiled again, as if
bothered by a pain.

"You don't think fifty thousand dulls is a lot of
money," Grom said.

Pop's eyes narrowed. Then he threw up his
hands. "You structure guards are all alike. All
alike. Jeez, you come right out with it, don't you?
Pow! Bang! Between the eyes." He lowered his
head and looked at the yellow smears on his plate.

He looked up. "Nossir. Fifty thou's chicken feed, if you must know. This is earth, Mr. Grom, not a cake sale. What'm I gonna do with you? Take you on walks? Window shopping? Look at it from my side a sec. I'm supposed to put you up, give you three changes of bed linen, feed you, give you a guide, and keep you entertained for three weeks. Billy here, she can earn fifty kay a day with a flusher, facryn! I don't know why they do this to me."

Billy served the continental breakfast: two slices of bread, a pat of butter, a disk of jam, a cup of coffee.

"Maybe I can stay in a hotel?" Grom suggested. He had a distinct sense that something was amiss.

Zow!" Pop cried. "Oh, zow! Are you ever green, kid. Ten kay a night in a cheap place. No food. Five days and you're flat."

"It may be better to spend five days on my own than to impose on you."

Now Pop's eyes narrowed again. He leaned back and searched for matches in his trouser pocket. He said:

"Well, Mr. Grom, I might be exaggerating a little, too. It's not so bad, fifty thou. Frugal, but enough. Right, Billy?"

Billy turned from the sink. "Sure, Pops."

"We'll show you a nice time, Mr. Grom. Just like it says here in the contract." He tapped the folder with a thick finger. "You keep your side of it, and we keep ours."

"In other words," Grom said, "it's better to have fifty thousand than nothing."

Pop shook his head. Then he lit his cigar. Puffing, he said: "They ever teach you about diplomacy, kid? Pow," he said, and he shook his head again.

"I'd like to be on my way," Grom said. "We're in the middle of a city here. I'd like to get out and see something."

"Billy, come here. Mr. Grom wants to plan his day." Billy joined them at the table. She pushed some plates aside and put her chin up on her hand.

"Well, sir?" Pop asked, "what's your pleasure? Sports? Hunting? Historical battles? Mountain climbing? You name it, we got it . . . while the dulls last, that is. Want to ride an elephant? Shoot a tiger? Dive for sponge? What's your thing outdoors?"

"All that around here?"

"Where else? Just a short trip by the undercrust."

"Well, for a start I'd just like to look around," Grom said. "I come from a water planet. I'd just . . . oh, maybe look at the prairie . . . birds . . ."

"Nature," Pop said matter-of-factly. He looked at the ash on his cigar. He gestured with it. "Very good choice. Excellent. Frugal. Sensible. Yessir. You keep that up, Mr. Grom, and we might just skinny by. Billy, you heard the gentleman. Nature it is. Take him to his first activity."

Grom asked: "How long a trip is that? Should I be ready for an overnight stay?"

"Nothing like that. Five minutes from here."

"Five minutes? Prairies around here? I thought we were quite a ways north-east."

Pop looked at Grom with some puzzlement. "I don't get you," he said. "We've got everything around here. Prairies, jungles, deserts, mountains, rivers, marshes. You name it, kid, we've got it . . . Just don't worry about it," he continued, seeing Grom's frown. He put his cigar down and slapped the table with both hands. "Off you go, children. The father of the house must go to work. I work at the pyramids. Ought to come see them. A nice, frugal activity, the pyramids." With that he rose. "Cheeruu," he called, and he waddled out, a short, fat little man.

THEY rode the undercrust toward the prairies. The crowded train rattled in a narrow tunnel creaking and squealing at the turns, now slow, now fast. People sat on benches, people stood. He and she hung on straps and swayed along with the car. He chewed beetle gum. Billy had insisted it was a real thrill and perkpopped you up scooroolishly in the ayem. It tasted sweet, then bitter. And judging by its effect on Billy, it colored the tongue red. It didn't perkpop him up, scooroolishly or otherwise.

He was still puzzled by the geographical question. He thought he understood something about earth geography. Like all others before him, he'd studied an old atlas in the *gorushka* library. This vast warren was the city of Eastcoast. The praries began a thousand mils southwest of here, in the Great Plains. Would he see a real prairie or just grasslands in the suburbs? Pop didn't inspire him with confidence. Was this a ruse to save money? He decided he'd see. Land was land. He needed to orient himself.

The undercrust was very old and rickety. It bumped and rocked. The lights went out for seconds at a time. But now the lights went out altogether, and the train ground to a halt; they were surrounded by eerie silence.

"Zoowishy," he heard Billy say. "A zonking power failure . . . Get your paws off me, fatso," she yelled at someone, and he heard a slapping sound; then there was a sound of motion. "Runs his hams up my leg, the pig. Never fails, Grommy . . . Say, Grommy, you interested in Sensuality? It's cheap, you know, what with all the Space Marines around here. More Sensy shops than any other. Go to a sensy shop, fatso!" she yelled at someone; "that's where you should go, not molesting working chicks."

He waited until her attention was, presumably, back on him. Then he asked: "What is Sensuality? What're you talking about?"

"Jeez," she cried, "are you people sheltered! You mean it? You don't know? Oh, wow! Half the trade that comes to earth comes for the Sensy shops, and you want to see a prairie!"

"Tell me," he said. "You've aroused my curiosity."

"It's an activity, silly," she said. "You know, sensuous experience. If you're worried about it being a sin, forget it, Grommy. It ain't. All fifteen hundred major churches have filed exemptions. You don't do anything, but it's scooroolish fun. I go sometimes on Sundays."

"But," he insisted, "what is it?"

Some of the people who stood around them, people who had enjoyed the exchange in silence, now snickered. He noticed a rise in the temperature. The cooling system had cut out. They must be deep underground.

"They sit you down and wire you up, you

know, just like for a tiger hunt, or something, and
then you can have a grand old time. Girls with
girls, boys with boys, girls with boys, girls with
dogs or bulls or . . . you know. They even have an
alien booth. And it's only two hundred a sesh."

"They wire you up," he said flatly.

"Yeah. Right into your nervysys. You feel it like
you're it. Wow! It's scooroolish good."

The lights came on and the car lurched into
motion.

"There he is, see him? That fat pig. Yeah, fatsy,
turn your head. Ought to be ashamed of yourself,
pawing a decent chick."

The object of her anger, a small portly man—
Grom remembered seeing him seated in front of
Billy—now stood some ways farther up. He hid
himself behind a newspaper. The people around
them smiled.

Grom was puzzled, disoriented. He meant to
ask her more about this business. He'd never
heard of such a thing and much of what she'd said
was incomprehensible. He'd understood the girls
with girls, boys with boys part of it. The rest was
obscure. He waited for the screeching wail of
wheels to stop. The train rounded a curve and ran
into a station. It rushed past waiting people on a
platform, then came to a halt.

"We're there," she said. "Keep with me."

She elbowed her way through the crowd,
through the crush of people trying to get in. She
waited on the platform while he followed. Then
she led the way. He dropped his beetle gum into a
pole-mounted basket as they passed it by.

They walked in a huge tunnel of concrete with
a crowd of sullen, preoccupied people. Pipes

passed overhead, and puddles of water or oil had accumulated at intervals. At spaced distances along the walls he saw uniform posters. Each said: "Pretty."

He pointed. "Those signs. What's the significance of that?"

"Sublimi ads." His puzzled face made her continue. "You *think* pretty, and the place *is* pretty."

"But this place is ugly," he protested. "Just look at it. Old pipes, puddles, dirty walls."

"You don't get it," she said. "It's pretty, don't you see? There. It says so," and she pointed to the signs.

Grom didn't know if he should take her seriously or not. She was a lively lass, but a little on the odd side. He expected that "Pretty" was a brand name, one she didn't know.

They walked in silence for a moment. Then he spotted, among the monotonous "Pretty" signs, one that said "Ugly."

"And that?" he asked. "What's that?"

"That's for variety, silly. Nothing's *just* pretty. That's not realistic."

FROM the large tunnel they passed into a shopping arcade. And from the arcade she led the way into a side street. She stopped before the entrance of a large, nondescript building. She looked in her purse at a slip of paper, inspected the sign above the entrance. It said, HOLOCOLOMBO N-58.

"Here we are," she announced, and she pushed her way into a revolving door beckoning Grom to follow. "Wait here," she said when they were inside the place. The foyer had red carpeting, wood-paneled walls, and dim yellow light from a chandelier. She was at a booth negotiating with a lady in glasses. Presently she was back, pointed to the left, and they were in motion.

Was this, he wondered, an elevator to the surface? He hadn't noticed that they had gained altitude since disembarking from the train. Nor, now that he thought about it, had he seen the sky since his arrival on earth. That would now be corrected.

Indeed, she led him into an elevator. She pushed some chits into a slot. The doors closed and they surged up. Then the doors opened, and there was the prairie, just a hallway away, behind glass, an immense expanse.

"Let's take a walk," she said. She opened a glass door, held it for him, and he passed out under the sky.

The sun was bright and the wind blew with some force. It bent the knee-high grass. It chased a few clouds across the sky. The smell was overpowering and sweet. He didn't know the names of these plants, but there was a profusion of them, and their scent was something very new.

He walked out a ways, brushing the grass with his hands. Land. So much open land. He'd never seen solidity from here to the horizon, a gentle rolling landscape, some small hills in the distance, a little village, tall storage tanks of some sort, and a truck on the highway half a mil to the left. He looked back at the glass-fronted building they'd just left, a one-story structure above the surface. To look at it, Grom couldn't have guessed the enormous underground complex below.

Billy had joined him, and he turned to her now.

"Beautiful," he said, "really lovely. I'll take you up on it. Let's go on a hike."

He strode out to his left, toward the highway. First he'd explore a bit. Then he'd collect some flowers for Marushka. Billy might know if the little village had a place to eat. They could have lunch there—

Grom suddenly found himself surrounded by darkness.

The shift was so sudden he caught his breath with a small exclamation. A sense of terror filled him, but it was dispelled when he heard Billy.

"Oh, croak," she cried. "Another power failure. Oh, Grommy, you should make them pay for this. They owe you double your money back *and* a free activity. All you have to do is fill out the forms. And your first time, too!"

His eyes became accustomed to the darkness. The darkness was not total. He could now make out glowing signs in four places. They said, EMERGENCY EXIT. The placement of the signs told him he was in a larger room, but not very large. Perhaps thirty meta in width, fifty long. He reached down to touch the vegetation. It was still there, but the wind had stopped blowing, and he could already sense the growing heat.

"Get me out of here, Billy," he said. "Let's go somewhere where we can see and talk. And then you tell me all about it. Every last bit."

"Zoowishy," she said, genuinely disappointed. "Zoo-zoowishy. I'm sorry, truly sorry. Your first activity. What a zonk."

"I HAVE the feeling that there's something about

earth I don't understand. Or maybe it's Cozy Pak Plan I don't understand. Or maybe you don't understand me."

They sat in a coffee shop at a two-seater table, she on the upholstered plasti-leather bench, he on the chair. The management provided a candle in a glass, whether for atmosphere or to anticipate power failure he didn't know. Probably the latter. For atmosphere the place relied on sublimi ads above the purple bench-backs: "Pleasant Service, Friendly Feeling." On either side of them were many two-man tables occupied by people eating lunch.

Billy smoked a cigarette she'd lit on the candle in the glass. It was oval in shape and very long and blended strictly for working chicks, the reason she didn't offer him one; besides she guessed he didn't smoke. They were called "Oh-Vuumbs."

"No," he said, when she began with "Jeez—," "don't tell me. Let me ask you some questions. But just answer the questions? Please?"

"It's your nicky, Grom-kid."

"What did I see back there?" He gestured vaguely.

"A nature activity."

"How'd they make it so real?"

"Holograph projections. Oh, Grommy, don't you know? Where did you come from, anyway?"

"Just answer the questions, Billy. Pretend I'm stupid. Why did you take me to that . . . activity? Why not to a real prairie or park?"

"Real?" she asked.

"Real. Real grass, real sky, real sun. Is it because you don't earn a commission on the real thing?"

She was offended, angry. Who'd he think he

was, insulting a working chick, etc., etc. plus a set of slangy exclamations and expletives. The real thing! Where'd he think he was? On a new planet? This is earth, Grom-kid.

"What do you mean . . . this is earth?"

"Kay," she said. "You *are* dumb. Ain't been any *real* thing on earth for centuries. You think our big skulls invented all this marvel stuff for fun? You realize what *one* Sensy booth costs to build? Forty-eight." She flicked ash angrily and fixed him with those green-lidded eyes. "Million. Four eight. Million. That's what. You can see it all here. Everything that's ever been on good old Mother Earth. All the old battles, all the sights. Pop told you he was Pyramids! Didn't you hear him? You can do it all, Grommy. *Fight* the battles, *thirst* in the Sahara, *sleep* with Merrilyroe, *eat* a shark, *be* eaten by a shark. You can eat a thousand meals and never take on a single calo. You want to be drunk and not be hung over? Milk a cow? Fall into a volcano? You can *do* it here, *feel* it, *see* it. The whole thing, Grommy, and you want the *real* thing!"

She was very offended.

"Zillion zillion trillion billion dulls or something. That's what it cost to build all this." Her hand swept around to indicate 'all this.' "Why'd you come here if you think it's all . . . nothing. The *real* thing!"

"I didn't say it was 'nothing,' " he soothed her. "I didn't *know,* is all. It's a custom in my tribe not to tell us what it is. Earth, I mean."

"Didn't anybody tell you? On the ship?"

"I hung about with other structure guards. I heard this and that, but I didn't put it together. I'm a simple man, Billy. Vizillo is a small, backward planet . . . Tell me, Billy. Is all of earth like this? An underground city? Does anybody live up on the surface?"

"Surface? Naw. It's dangerous up there. No life at all."

"And Africa, Euras, Astra? Cities like this on those continents? All with these activity theaters?"

She shook her head and turned to a serving girl who had appeared and stared at them grimly. Her starched apron had rust stains; her black skirt was short over fat rumps. "A skinnibug and a glass of Mu for me, Chick. Grommy? The same." The waitress left, having said nothing at all.

"Nothing on the other continents?"

"The only city on earth is Eastcoast, and Eastcoast has everything that's ever been. Only better."

"Excuse me, Mister, I overheard you say you come from Vizillo. I meant to ask you—"

"Hands off, freak, he's mine by contract. Back to your soupy-soup and mind!"

Billy spoke sharply to the man at the neighboring table, a skinny fellow in a turtleneck. He had a day's growth of beard. He'd leaned over, had put a hand on their table.

"I'm sure the gentleman can speak for himself, chick."

"Oh, no you don't!" Billy bristled. "Nossir! Grom-sock, tell this mooch to skoot off."

Grom shrugged and looked at the man. "I don't know the customs here. I don't mean to offend, but . . . skoot off."

"Scavengers!" Billy scolded. "Not enough to go

around as it is, for decent folk. Eight million people, three million visitors, less than one for three, if you read me, Grommy. And the big tour shops steal most of those. Little people can't make it any more. There's talk of advertising all the activities. They say there'll be directories and all. Pop and I couldn't make it then."

"There is no Mom?"

"Mom couldn't take it. She blasted off-planet when I was a sock."

"How do you make a living?"

"It's like this, you see," she said. "Only the guides know where all the places are. We take the mark—" She stopped and gave him a glance, started over. "We take the guest to the places where he wants to go. We get a little cut. But the big tour shops are taking over. They bring a hundred people at a crack, cut the commissions. We get squeezed. And you can't just blaze off like that. What'd we do off-planet? Pop and I? All we know is the activities. And guys like this cut in on you, tell the guest they know some place the guides don't know about. You get it both ways. Pow! like Pop says. Between the eyes."

Grom sensed her dilemma and began to feel sad for her, but he rose up above the emotion out of old habit. Pity destroyed *bal*.

"You're a super guide, Billy. You'll make it," he said.

"Jeez," she cried, pleased. "How can you say that? Your first activity and I blew it."

"You're great at explaining and you know everything," he said. "Tell me, Billy, of my fifty thousand, how much will you earn?"

"Six hundred and ninety-six," she said at once.

"The ninety-six is for your keep, the six hundred is commissions."

"And what if I don't go to any activities?"

Her face fell. "Zoowish," she cried. "What'd you do?"

"I don't know, but I want to ask you that too. Would you get some money, commissions?"

"How?" she asked. "No activity, no commission. It's your nicky, Grommy. You spend it, you keep it. It's up to you."

She was very gloomy.

"I don't have any money. You've got it. A letter of credit, I think they called it in the folder."

"It's still yours. You can cash it all in, if you want to. Any office of Banco Galactico will give you the loot in bills."

He mused over that for a second.

"You don't want to do that, Grom-sock. You won't have anything to do. You'll wander through the pretty corridors and look at shops just like those you've got at home . . ." Her voice was small. She dug into her purse for Oh-Vuumbs.

"I expect to have plenty to do," he said. "And I'll make sure that you're not hurt, no matter what I do."

She was unsure. She looked away from him. "Where are those skinnies?" she asked. "I'm starved . . . I blew it," she said, and she blew smoke at the candle. "Your first activity, and they short it out. Oh, mush."

He reached out and touched one of her hands. "Listen, Billy. It wasn't your fault. And besides, I didn't come to earth to go to movies."

"They aren't movies!" she protested, but he cut her off, squeezing her hand.

"Listen, Billy. Movies, holograms, it's all the same. I want to go to the surface."

"Wow," she cried. "You must be reeling."

The expression on her face was so astonished, he decided to drop the subject for the moment.

INSTEAD, to give her a pleasure, Grom agreed to try another activity in the afternoon.

This time nothing would go wrong.

They'd get away from Nuyo burrow where the power always failed. Wadicy station was much better, she suggested. Did he know? Wadicy had been a great capital in the ancient days. It'd been called The Great American Dream, though search her why an empire would be called that. All that was left of the ancients was part of a radiation bunker. And guess what? Billy's eyes lit up. She warmed to the subject. She displayed her know-how with evident pleasure. In a glass case in the bunker Grom could see the last surviving imperial book; not a fax, not a reconstruct, the real thing. It was the report of a commission on some important subject. "See," she said, "I know some things that aren't activities. But first we'll take in something real scooroolish, kay?"

They discussed what he should do munching the skinnies and sipping Mu through straws. Grom was used to fish fare and life-produced protein. The skinny tasted like space-ship food and had been grown in a yeast tank. He didn't want to disappoint his guide by asking any questions about its origins.

First she explained the difference between static and dynamic. She used one hand, holding a bite-disfigured skinny, to indicate the one; the other hand, which held the Mu, to indicate the other.

Static was what he'd already seen. You walked about in them and looked.

Dynamic was where they wired you up.

Dynamic was what he'd have to try. She insisted on it.

In the midst of a long listing of different activities, to each of which he reacted neutrally at best, she suddenly cried:

"I've got it, Grom-kid! I've got it. I'll take you to a potpourri!" But then her face fell. "Aw, I guess not—it'll run you a mint. Pops'll skin me." Then her face brightened again. "But its the greatest zapperoo there is, Grom. If you like Dynamic, that is."

"If you say so, Billy, I'll take you to a potpourri."

"Me?" she protested. "You can't do that. That'll wipe you out." She lowered her eyes. "I've never been to one before. Cause of that." She looked up. "Ten," she said, fixing him with green-lidded eyes. "Thousand. For you and me. Together."

Grom laughed. "It's only money, Billy. Let's go."

Wadicy was an hour away. They got there in a much better train. It rode on air, went deeper and faster, and they had to strap themselves into cushioned seats. All the way there, Billy fluctuated between delicious dread at the prospect and eager expectation. Grom gathered that potpouri was not only scooroolish, it was also zanyshivereeee!

The show lasted long hours, and in the process

the day fled. They emerged in the early evening.
They were both silent for a long time.

"I've never been through this before," she said
at last. They stood on the platform waiting for the
train. "You were sweet to buy me a chit. Potpourri
is a trip. A real trip. But I don't think I'd ever do it
again. It's too much. It makes you feel old. Afterwards, you know."

He nodded but didn't say anything.

In the Wadicy potpourri theater, you could re-
live the entire life of a man, a woman. The spe-
cialty was ancient history. You could be the man,
the woman of that time. It all began with birth and
ended in death. In the four hours that intervened
came the cargo of a lifetime's feeling, a flashing of
vast events—loves, hatreds, strivings, failures,
the hubris of success, the dread of loneliness and
neglect, infirmity, sickness, destitution, charity,
senility, the end.

Grom had been a journalist who'd become a
soldier, then a general in a terrible war. He was in
China and Arabia, in Washington, in Paris, all
around the globe. He negotiated a peace that
wouldn't hold. He had sweethearts and a wife and
a child killed by napalm in a campus riot. He
wrote a book. He was a member of a cabinet. A
madman gunned him down in front of a court
house but he recovered with one arm lame. A
committee investigated him for corruption; he
was guilty, found blameless, yet forced to resign.
He became religious and rose high in the ranks of
a new church; but he lost all of his conversion love
in vicious hierarchical fights. He was banished to
an island and ministered to primitives. A shark bit

off his lower legs when he dived for sponges to supplement his income. As he grew old, a native matron ruled him and ruled in his name with small-eyed cruelty. He tried to escape and on the fourth try succeeded. He died on a raft on the ocean in an ecstasy. He thought he was God.

Grom had left the building empty. He was not himself. The calm sense of *bal* was gone or stirred to such an extent he couldn't orient himself in the world. Like water in a jostled bucket, so his emotions slapped the sides of his soul and spilled over. He was two people: Grom Gravok, structure guard, and that strange adventurer, so filled with titanic desire, John Singer of the potpourri. The two couldn't be reconciled. The tension lamed him.

The real thing? Whatever it was that he'd experienced, it was the equivalent of reality.

He didn't know who Billy had been or what she had experienced; but the effect of the potpourri on her was much the same.

They rode home in silence, strapped into cushioned seats, lost in ancient yet very recent memories.

GROM went to bed in the narrow room, next to the decommissioned washing machine, the stand with old clothing, certain that by morning he would be normal again. He awoke eight hours later still disturbed by the very real presence within him of another person, John Singer. His nervous system couldn't distinguish between the two sets of memory. But Grom Gravok, the structure guard, had gained a little strength. He knew he had to get away from here somehow. He had to find himself again. He yearned for the serenity of *bal*, trembled with basic anxiety. No gravitron drums turned anywhere on earth. Still he knew that he couldn't have heard the "little ones." And that knowledge made him extremely nervous. His body shuddered with dread. Structure collapse could be advancing all around him, without his knowledge.

A strangely serious, taciturn Billy took him to a branch of the Banco Galactico. She said nothing while he cashed in his letter of credit; not a word of protest escaped her. She had also changed her appearance. Her lips, eyelids were no longer painted. She had washed the curls from her hair. She wore a wide skirt and a sweater. She had neglected to squirt perfume behind her ears, in the crook of her arms.

Thirty-three thousand dulls were left in his account. He folded the blue bills away into a zippered pocket of his suit.

Over breakfast in an eatery, he told her what he wanted to do.

She took note of it, thought for a moment, checked her watch; then she explained how they would proceed. They went home and packed over night bags; she left a recorded message for Pop; then they caught an undercrust local to another station and arrived just in time for the only transcontinental train of the day. He put their bags in the overhead rack, her blue one next to his red one with the stencilled words—Time Collapse Intragalactica. They strapped themselves in and were soon in motion. A very slow start, almost a creeping, became a headlong rush as the train descended very deep into the bedrock on its air-cushioned course.

JOHN SINGER had experienced his conversion in a small cabin, in an out-of-the-way valley of the Rocky Mountains, near a town called Henderson, in what had then been called the State of Colorado.

He had retired there for a long vacation after his ouster from the government. He went there to lick his wounds, to think things over. The cabin belonged to a friend of his. It was remote and primitive. Singer had to fetch his water from a well and to burn wood in a stove to keep warm.

Grom Gravok had experienced Singer's conversion as if it had been his own. For a few months, a very few months, Singer had felt what Grom considered a natural state, the peace of *bal*, although Singer had called it by another name. That segment of experience united the two personalities. Singer caught in the gossamer threads of spirit and Grom Gravok in his natural state were basically the same man.

When Grom had awakened the morning after his experience of the potpourri, two distinct urges had impelled him to go to the surface. He wished to be free of Singer's oppressive psychic presence, and to do so he thought he must see for himself the spot where God's finger had touched that ancient. At the same time, Grom wished to see earth, the real earth, not an underground city. Eastcoast and structures had too much in common. Grom longed above all for the sustaining, subtle support of the *gorushka*. If he couldn't get that, he wanted solitude.

He learned from Billy that one could still go to the mountains. Earth had its outposts all about this and the other continents—small groups of people who watched the planet and charted the storms that raged above, sampled the atmosphere, measured crust tremors, dipped probes into the sea. Slowly chaos pressed in upon the remnant of humanity. The outposts watched the steady progress of the inevitable.

Someday, Billy had said, there would be no more people on earth. The oxygen will have been fixed.

They hurtled toward one of these outposts. Den Station in the Rorange.

The train drove deeply under the continent in a tunnel carved by plasma and shaped like a slack hose, one end attached to Eastcoast the other to the underside of the mountains. The train fell down, almost, moved by gravity. The inertial energies of the fall carried them up again toward the surface as the tunnel turned up.

"So they did learn to do it after all," John Singer thought, thinking with Grom's mind; or was this Grom's thought reflecting Singer's memories? In Singer's day such trains were seen as utopian dreams. "Some utopia," John Singer thought, reflecting on Grom Gravok's memories. Or was it the other way about?

Grom found it confusing to be two men. But Singer's memories were useful. He understood a great deal now he hadn't grasped before.

They fell for two hours and rose for two hours.

Grom felt no discomfort. His body was accustomed to all kinds of gravitational effects. Billy seemed unwell on the way down, but she stirred into life on the ascent when the natural gravity bit into their bodies and they could unstrap and move about.

"You're my last visitor," she announced suddenly after a long silence, stirring coffee a girl had brought them on a tray.

"Oh?"

"I haven't lived," she said seriously; her entire manner was different now. She was resolute and determined. "I didn't know it before, but now I do. I'm leaving earth and heading outward, just like Mom."

"How'll you do that? I thought you were . . ." Grom didn't want to say "poor."

"I'll find a way," she stated. "Mary always did!"

"Mary?"

"Mary O'Gronsky. Mary never hesitated. She'd just step right out, right into the darkness. Something always happened."

"I take it Mary O'Gronsky was the girl whose life you . . . ?"

She nodded, lips over a raised cup. She set the cup down and took a puff on her cigarette.

"I'm very big," she said. "I've seen many things. Earth is too small for me. Jeez, Grom," she cried, and the momentary flash of enthusiasm recalled for a second the Billy he knew, "you've no idea how big the world is. And here I was, hustling in a very narrow track, day after day— vaccu the place Saturday mornings, a Sensy show on Sunday afternoon, and grinding, grinding on the old circuit. I'm twenty-eight," she said; he didn't know if it was an accusation, a boast, or a statement. "Never!" she said. "Never again." She looked at him as if she expected contradiction.

But Grom said nothing. Her stare recalled another woman, his wife (John Singer's wife), who on the occasion of her twenty-eighth birthday (they were flying to the Bahamas for a vacation) had quarrelled with him (with John Singer) about the number of children they'd have—she'd wanted none. Joan had been a criminal lawyer. She'd divorced him after she gave birth to Annie. Marushka wanted five children, all boys.

He fell into a reverie about Joan and Marushka and Annie all intertwined while Billy went on, asserting her own future, expanding its proportions, explaining the many alternate paths that lay before her still, each beckoning for exploration, despite the fact that she had nothing, was twenty-eight, and couldn't possibly imagine the first step toward her goal. But Mary never let herself be stopped. Mary blasted rock when the way was barred. Yessir!

Den Station in the Rorange received them with suspicion. They had been the only passengers on the train to disembark there. A man had to unlock a gate to let them into the building from the platform. He asked them to come to his office, which they did; Grom carried their bags—her blue one and his red one. The man sat down behind the desk, took off his glasses, polished them, and asked what their business was here. They stood before him, hadn't been asked to sit down.

Grom felt strong, overpowering irritation. He was John Singer, not Grom Gravok. Grom would have suppressed such emotions long before they could gather force.

"I want to take a look at the surface," he said with a voice devoid of any supplication.

Well, now, the man replied. Slowly, a little slowly, here. Did Mr . . . ? Mr. Gravok have the requisite permits from DOS? (DOS, Billy whispered, was the Department of Safety.) Without such a permit, of course, the trip had been wasted. The man breathed on the lense of his glasses and, polishing, looked up.

"I don't have any permits, so I guess you'll just have to make them out, here and now."

"Me?" the man said, incredulous. He put on his glasses to see this person better. "Me? Mr. Gravok, you labor under an immense delusion—"

Grom turned purple. "Get on your feet, creep!" he thundered, entirely possessed by another. "Who do you think you're addressing, anyway? Can't you recognize a cabinet official when you see one? Start writing or you'll regret you ever laid eyes on me."

The little man, whom John Singer (if not Grom Gravok) had recognized as a minor bureaucrat, came to his feet. Behind the eyes now showed fear. He murmured apologies. He hesitated. Then he sat down again, dove into a drawer for some forms, and began to write hastily. It was his job to act quickly. Discrete inquiries could be made afterward or, better yet, not at all.

Minutes later, armed with forms and instructions about the whereabouts of lifts, Grom and Billy were in yet another concrete corridor. Grom's face was still an angry frown.

"Cabinet official?" Billy asked.

He looked at her. He was jolted, confused. "I
. . . I . . ." He gave it up and simply shook his
head. In truth he was moritified by his aggressive
behavior, and his body pulsed with the unaccustomed discharge of hormones he hadn't known he
had, and he longed to be rid of John Singer and the
terrifying slavery of John Singer's compulsive
drive. Was this what they called freedom?

From a large encavement on which numerous
buildings fronted and from which other corridors
led in all directions, they took a righthand path to
a smaller square. Here they entered a facility
where attendants equipped them with suits,
masks, and auxiliary oxygen devices. They
signed for small homing radios, were given maps.
They affixed their signatures to liability waivers
that freed Den Station of any responsibility
should they be lost. They paid the lift fee of five-
fifty each. Then they were shown to the elevators
and went up, very high up, in Grom's estimation;
which was a way of saying that they'd been very
deep undercrust. And then, from a dark and narrow concrete bunker, he stepped out to the
surface—the real surface this time, not a holographic mirage.

AND he saw nothing at all.

Or rather, he found himself in a violent wind
storm. The wind blew, blasted, raced, cut,
shrieked by him at an unbelievable velocity. It
tugged him, pulled him, jerked him and yet
pressed him back. The wind was laden with very
fine yellow dust. In seconds it powered over his
suit and visor. Despite the tightness of the suit, a
bitter taste formed in his mouth. He wiped his

visor and saw yellow, hurtling yellow all about
him.

Grom turned back. He barely saw Billy in her
dark blue suit. She stood uncertainly in the low
bunker's rectangular opening. He stepped back
and took her hand. Then, together, they pressed
into the wind.

He felt her resistance almost at once. Her body
seemed to tremble, and the trembling came to him
through her hand, through the glove. He held her
left. With her right hand she fumbled on the but-
tons of her belt-mounted communications pack.
The noise was so great that unaided speech was
impossible.

Static crackled. "Oh, Grom, I'm scared!" he
heard her say.

"Hold tight. You're safe. This wind must be
gusting. It should relent. Let's walk a little."

He pulled her along, carefully feeling his way
over rough, rocky terrain while she repeated that
she was terrified.

The wind *was* gusting. From time to time its
intensity subsided, and then they saw churning
clouds and swirls of yellow dust laced with
brown dust and whitish dust and black spirals of
dust.

Whenever the wind took a breath, she seemed
to relax a little.

They walked on, slowly, and as time passed he
felt the wind die. Suddenly it stopped. It left vast
tons of dust in the air which now began to settle
slowly like a very fine misty rain.

As fog lifts so the dust settled. Minute by minute the view cleared. At first they saw dark, grey
rock to the right. Then more rock piled behind

that, and rock above that. It rose higher and higher. It was wild, eroded, chiseled rock, mountains sliced thin and ground to circular posts, flat tables, intricate traceries that recalled hot lead poured into water.

But it was the endless plain to their left which caused Billy to panic. Like Grom she had watched the dust veil drop over the remnants of Rorange. Then they both turned in the other direction. Here was a limitless expanse of dust arranged in fantastic, numberless, sharp-edged dunes. Very far in the distance a falling veil of dust percipitated down from a yellow sky.

And from that direction they now saw the lightning-rapid advance of another fist of wind. It punched through the veil and ripped through the dunes. It came toward them, a dark ball of elemental force, driving planetary sediment.

Billy screamed, turned, and ran toward the bunker, whose roof was unevenly laden with dust as if with snow. She stumbled and fell. She clawed herself upright. Grom heard her sobbing panic over the radio. She ran for the safety of the little concrete outjutting. He followed her slowly, already battered by the wind.

Billy cowered, sobbing, by the elevator, her clumsy gloves placed in pleading on the door.

He tried to coax her back to rationality, but she was beside herself, incoherent, and utterly panicked. At last he rang for the lift. When it arrived he half pulled, half carried her on.

They went back down.

THE following morning Grom said good-bye to Billy at the train station.

They shook hands, and he handed her the little blue overnight bag. On an impulse she embraced him and pecked a kiss on his cheek. Her eyes glistened.

"I'll never forget you, Gromkid," she said; her voice was husky. "You've given me a new life."

He shook his head. "God be with you, Billy. I gave you and you gave me. Such is life. Now follow through. Do it. Get away."

"I will," she sobbed.

"Like Mary would. Courage. Don't be held up by anything."

"I promise."

A girl-attendant at the train's door beckoned. Billy looked at him again. She shook her head, filled with emotion. Then she turned and got on. She waved to him as the train pulled away.

"Zoowishy," he murmured to himself, smiling. "Zoo-zoowishy."

Then he went back to the hotel.

He inspected the gear he had bought the day before, following that abortive stay on the surface: a tent, a mattress, a carrypack; food rations, a moisture-capture, a stove; rope, heavy socks, thermal underwear; a compass, maps, a strong radio; and various other odds and ends suggested by John Singer's memories or a store clerk torn between pleasure at Grom's big purchase and wonder at the visitor's overvaulting madness.

Grom packed his gear, shouldered the load, and set out for the surface again.

He had resolved to spend his remaining time up there, in the awesome wildnerness of the surface. He'd known he'd do it in that moment of stillnes when the dust had settled revealing the Mother

Planet's ravaged face. Alone, up there, seeking *bal*.

He had bought the gear alone, unaided, Billy had been hysterical. He'd taken her to a room in Den Station's only hotel aided by a heavyset matron with warts and a nearly full mustache. And when the officious, suspicious matron had at last left them alone, he'd consoled Billy in a way John Singer would have approved and that Mary O'Gronsky had known how to appreciate. He'd told Billy of his intentions as they lay together watching an artificial sunset projected on the wall. Then he'd gone shopping. After breakfast the next morning, he gave her twenty-five thousand dulls—so that she might get free and fulfill her dream, or Mary O'Gronsky's dream, or both. Grom didn't care. In his life money didn't matter; nor did John Singer give a damn. Singer had created fortunes and he'd lost them, like the snap of a finger. To Singer money was a means. Grom kept enough to get home. He already had a ticket. Or if he chose to wander, enough for a start somewhere. The rest would manifest somehow.

Whether he'd go back to Vizillo or head out for parts unknown—that was the question he'd answer up there.

Bal would tell him. If he couldn't find *bal*, he probably wouldn't come back down again.

THE wind howled and then it settled again. It rolled up ten thousand carpets of dust and flung them into the sky. Sometimes it was still for days on end. In the sky tiny particles of silicate drew sunshine into multichrome reflections. Sometimes water clouds filled the sky and it rained; it mudded. Torrents of mud ran. Rivers of mud; angry, yellow-foamed rivers that bared the rock, that boiled and roared and fell over the cliffs with a thunder of a few hours and a slow, oozing drip of days.

Grom wandered.

He went up, into the Rorange. He saw forests of petrified wood. He saw art so strange only the unencumbered freedom of wind blast could create it over centuries. He saw lakes and pools whose water was bitter. He saw tough, rocklike vegetable scum clinging for dear life to rock, to occasional mudriver beds. He saw needles of stone and spires of stone and temples of stone. He saw boulders balanced on needles of stone and needles balanced on boulders.

He wandered, but with a system.

He sought with compass and map the spot where John Singer had been touched by the Divine finger. There was no practical sense in the search. Since Singer's day the Rocky Mountains had been so utterly changed Grom didn't recognize the place nor the maps that gave him an overview. He couldn't be sure where that spot was. There was no common point of reference except Den Station, in Singer's day a major city. One point. Not enough except to aid a guess. Yet Grom searched. He knew he'd know the spot. And if it wasn't *really* the spot, it didn't matter. God was everywhere. He interpenetrated this dimension. The value of the exercise was that it gave Grom things to do—map study in the tent at night, compass readings in the day time, measuring and charting with a grease pencil on a plastic overlay.

He reached the spot on the tenth day out. He

camped near the edge of a funnel-shaped valley, a triple column of stone behind him, the remnants of Tomichi mountain (he guessed). Across the funnel was a wall of rock. It seemed he remembered that wall. In Singer's days it had been higher and pines had run like a line of soldiers right to the edge of it. An over-eager soldier or two had tumbled down and caught himself in cracks and crevices. That red was the ancient red. That grey was a nose shape the ancient nose.

He stayed for three weeks. Or possibly only for three days. Time was meaningless here. He wandered about. He ranged far from his camp. Slowly, very slowly, he began to feel like himself again.

After ten days, or possibly two, he got the notion that he'd find a souvenir for Marushka. This mission began to fill his waking hours. He searched and searched. Something very, very ancient. Something of real value. Something they'd encase in clear glass and place next to the *gorushka* shrine in their cubohome. Something that would be a memento of his Maturity Trip and yet a gift from him to her. Something they'd show to the five children Marushka wanted, all five of them boys, all five structure guards with clear ears for the lisp of gravitron.

He wandered about with a small pick axe and dug here and there, lifting and piling the dust—loose on top, packed deeper, then almost the solidity of rock down below. For a long time he found nothing.

Then one day he lifted a flat-pressed cake of dust and saw the corner of a something with a dull, metallic sheen. He freed the something. It was a piece of light, maleable metal ironed flat by pressure. Aluminum, by the feel and look. Once it might have been cylindrical in shape. It was only part of a cylinder, torn from a cylinder. The pressure had forced wrinkles into the surface.

He carried his find to the tent. He washed it with sweet water from the moisture-capture. He polished it with one of his heavy socks. He examined it in the beam of a flashlight. With tremendous joy and excitement he then saw the faded trace of very ancient letters. Singer's memories allowed him to decipher the sound. The letters, a mere discoloration on the metal, a faint but unmistakeable impression or chemical change on the surface, said "Coca ola." Faintly Grom seemed to recall the significance of the words, but his Singer-self was receeding. The new yet ancient memories did not come as readily any more. All that was left of Singer was a feeling—a strange, troubled, sad feeling of something that had longed, hated, suffered, and passed on.

He wrapped the metal in one of his shirts. He tied a rope about the shirt to secure the metal. He placed the shirt at the bottom of his pack. Then he cooked himself a meal on the stove and went to bed on his mattress.

The next day he awoke with dawn. The day was still. The sun gleamed in the silicate suspension of the air.

Grom distinctly felt in his heart the peace of *bal*. A limpid harmony.

He broke camp and set out for home.

THE rest was a movement in reverse. A long journey through the wilderness. A descent into the underworld. A train ride in a tunnel shaped like a slack hose.

He called Billy by visiphone. A recorded voice told him she was no longer listed at that code.

He splurged on a cab ride to the space port.

El-tuná received him. He hopped about on the lunar surface for a day. Then the TC Liner *Belfortuna* carried him over fifty parsecs from Earthmoon to Vizillo.

At the space port a delegation of the *gorushka* waited to receive him, all elders, mostly of his own age. His father and uncles were among them. His mother, sisters, and Marushka were there, but they stood back, away from the men.

He looked at the elders and saw anxious expectation on their faces. He ran toward them, a red bag over his shoulder with the words Time Collapse Intragalactica stenciled on it in white. He embraced them and shook hands and greeted them. One of the men said:

"Grom, brother. So good to have you back. But tell us, what did you think of . . . earth? The big world? What was it like?"

Grom examined his questioner and sensed worry in the man's voice. He realized then that he too must act like an elder and say the traditional words, the words that hid so much agonizing experience under a blessing.

"Splendid," he said. "Splendid freedom. Oh, earth is magnificent. The land, the mountains, the prairies. It's the beginning, Tushka, and it's the end."

The elders beamed. Grom broke through them and ran to Marushka.

THE EASTCOAST
CONFINEMENT

I

IT WAS the summer of 2008, a perfectly ordinary year, but for the sake of context you should know that it was the ninth year of New Harmony and seventh of the first and original penal reservation, the Eastcoast Confinement.

On July 15th of that year, at 7:19 in the morning, Berlin's Superintendent of Police boarded Lufthansa's Flight 103 for the transatlantic trip to Eastcoast—and lest Karl Schmidt think that the Senate took his trip lightly, it sent a delegation of its senior members to the airport despite the early hour, who followed him all the way to the end of the ramp urging his objective, careful, and professional assessment of the American experience.

Karl Schmidt undertook the voyage yielding to pressure of the worst sort. He was fifty-nine and four years beyond retirement age, a fact that the Senate had at last turned to its advantage, suggesting through intermediaries that, should he continue obstinate and old-fashioned, the Senate could and would replace him with a man more modern in his outlook. But they hoped they wouldn't have to.

Schmidt stood before the senators, tall, grave, his long face somewhat longer than usual, his sparse grey hair combed back straight with a part in the center. He assured them that he'd do his best. "But gentlemen," he said at the end, "don't think that a single visit will change my mind. Old dogs don't learn new tricks, and I've always opposed aping the Amis. Their solutions turn out to be tomorrow's problems."

Just then they heard the muffled report of an explosion somewhere on the airport grounds. Soon thereafter a voice announced yet another major sabotage attempt. Fortunately it had miscarried. With the exception of an old bus, no damage had been done to man or property.

The senators looked pointedly at Herr Schmidt, and he in turn shrugged his shoulders. The men would be caught. Justice would be done. A few hotheads, anarchists, and antisocials shouldn't panic society to adopt the drastic American solution. Schmidt understated the problem, of course. It was pretty grim in Europe. He himself sometimes felt desperation as he watched Western Society unravel before his eyes. But nothing could convince him that Confinements were the answer. The senators obviously disagreed. He saw it in their eyes. Schmidt is too old and set in his ways, they thought. Too bad he is a public institution in Berlin and difficult to shunt aside without political pain.

OVER THE Atlantic, in the perpetual sunshine of

high altitude, Schmidt reflected on past and future.

Since his birth in 1949, the world had transformed itself under the twin pressures of growing population and shrinking energy supplies. It had all turned out differently than he'd thought it would, in his early twenties, when world catastrophe had been predicted. Instead the world had carried on, creaking and groaning like an old weary ship, too stupid to know that it should sink. Atomic war had been avoided, but in its stead had come disorders all over the globe—not least of which had been the Chino-Russian war of '79, an incongruously bright period in Schmidt's life, for he had served in the International Intervention Brigade and, incidentally, had trained in the U.S. before the IIB was mobilized. Then in 1999 came the disaster some people said Nostradamus had predicted. It hadn't been a man-made holocaust but a geological happening that had reduced the islands of Japan to the Keys of Japan in a series of convulsions and had pulled much of California into the sea. Flooding on a scale unheard of since Noah had lightened the planet's human cargo, and men still cleared debris after nearly a decade. China was now once again the spoil of warlords who paid a kind of distracted allegiance to the ghost of the People's Republic. Russia was the Sick Man of Asia, preoccupied in putting down internal revolts. Europe had fragmentized into thirty-five sovereignties, and the fragments had been gathered into the union of Europe ruled from the cantons of Switzerland, presumably safe from the sea. And America had become a theocracy of sorts.

The United States were now Harmonies or New Harmony or simply Harmony. The regime called itself the New Puritan Secular Order. NPSO was the brainchild of a single man, one Ralph Waldo Gunnison, a tiny, withdrawn, wispy figure who'd spent forty years as an obscure teacher of Mental Science at night while repairing TV sets by day. He reached prominence in 1978 as leader of the Meditation Crusade. His object was simple enough. He saw preparations for the Intervention and proposed an alternative. Let the American people pray and meditate, and let the boys stay home. He theorized that Mind could grab hold of Substance in deep prayer and thus force its desire into Manifestation. Let Americans pray for peace on the Mongolian border. The force of Spirit could overcome the force of the Sword. This appealed to a population torn by Vietnam II (which was really Laos I). Gunnison became a pest in the Senate, organized protests against the Intervention, and predicted awesome disasters when the nation went off to war again. The natural disaster came in '99, two years after the Peace of Tchu-Peh. It coincided with a severe recession and other disorders. Gunnison became the first Harmonizer, and the New Puritan Secular Order was launched.

Karl Schmidt had passed through the United Harmonies in 2001 on his way to Brasilia, which had emerged as a dominant force in world politics, inadvertenly filling a vacuum created up north of it. International conferences now tended to be held—if they were held in the New World— in San Paulo or Brasilia. No one liked prudish Miami, prissy New Francisco, or drab Eastcoast. The changes had been visible then, but nothing like he expected to see now. Mind had indeed transformed Substance and made Manifest a world in Ralph Waldo's image and likeness. And the people loved it. The world wanted to emulate it. And people of Berlin lusted after harmony, tired of the social disease, the dissolution of order and meaning, that plagued all erstwhile industrialized countries—except America, of course.

Uniformed girls served lunch a little ahead of Schmidt's accustomed meal time. He picked at the food but ordered three bottles of wine anticipating a dry time in Eastcoast. Then he opened his slender briefcase and took out the briefing materials for a second perusal. After a while he laid the papers aside and shook his head much as he'd done some days ago in his widower apartment in the blue-plush armchair beside the empty paraqueet cage by the window where he did evening work. He couldn't reconcile himself to the notion of confinements. He wondered at the brazen boldness of the erstwhile TV repairman who'd dared launch a social experiment of unprecedented proportions and unpredictable consequences. Yes, Schmidt expected that consequences would flow from this sooner or later, despite claims to the contrary made in the Harmony brochures.

In such musings and under the mellow influence of rhenish, Karl Schmidt dozed off. A stewardess lifted his head and gently slipped a pillow beneath it without his notice. He slept soundly until the plane began its descent.

THE plane approached low over water. In the distance to the right brightly painted sailboats

swayed unevenly in waves created by a small
tugboat bound out to sea. The plane moved over
solid ground. The wheels touched down and the
engines reversed. The green blur became im-
maculately combed lawn, and up ahead large
white billboards with blue lettering came toward
them as they rolled forward. Soon he could read
the signs. Meditation, Substance, Manifestation.
Karl Schmidt had arrived in New Harmony. They
taxied to the gate, and a voice announced the local
time and welcomed them to Peaceful Abiding
International Airport.

Schmidt gathered his hat and briefcase. He
lined up with others on one of the five aisles of the
jumbo and deplaned past the tired smile-masks of
the girls. To him this was and would remain Ken-
nedy International, the airport where he had arrived on his first trip to the United States, a young
man mesmerized by dreams of adventure and
tired of the Vice Squad in Berlin. He'd been bound
for an Oklahoma training field of the International
Intervention Brigade but had stopped a while in
New York City to taste the forbidden fruits of MJ
and Synthesex—legal in the States, but at that
time, still prohibited in Germany. Schmidt was
sure that no one smoked marijuana now in Harmony, and the orgasmic sex-drug that had been
all the rage in the late '70s was surely taboo.

The letter of invitation had promised him a
full-time guide and aide, a certain Richard H.
Gilligan, executive assistant to Eastcoast's Commissioner of Police. Schmidt walked out through
the mobile gate peering ahead at the people who'd
come to meet the flight. A youngster in a bright
red jacket with a blazer caught his eye. He had a

pink, scrubbed, wholesome look, a reddish crew cut, a freckled face. The youngster saw Schmidt's searching look and moved toward him with the hesitant expectation of a man greeting a relative stranger. "Herr schmidt?" "Mr. Gilligan?" The young man's hand came forward and gave his a tight, manly grip.

"Welcome to Harmony, Herr Schmidt. Welcome to Eastcoast. You have a good flight? I sure hope you did; we want you to be happy with us. Get off to a good start, and all that. Herr Schmidt, have *we* got things to show *you!*"

The young man was tense, apparently, and he effused when he was tense.

"I am very curious, of course," Schmidt said evenly. "I'm sure it'll be interesting."

"I'll say!" Gilligan enthused. "You better believe it, Herr Schmidt."

In an attempt to ease the young man's tension, Schmidt said: "Perhaps we better make that 'Karl' from now on."

"Sure, Karl, anything you say, sir. Just call me Hank. Name's Richard H., you know. The H. stands for Henry, and that comes out Hank. I don't use 'Richard.' Haven't used 'Richard' since I joined the force. The boys kid you too much. They call you 'Dick Dick' and things like that. You know what I mean? Dick? Detective?"

Schmidt nodded gravely. "I understand you perfectly, Hank."

"This way, please, Karl, if you'll just follow me . . ."

They walked through an echoing hall. Schmidt noted the aseptic order and the unparalleled neatness. He recalled a tourist poster he'd seen on the Kurfuerstendam: WE MAKE SWITZERLAND LOOK DOWNRIGHT DIRTY. VISIT THE HARMONIES. Nowadays, of course, it took little to exceed Switzerland in cleanliness. It was the hub of the European Union and something of a moral as well as aesthetic slum.

They moved toward the male side of the Customs line. Gilligan was pleased that the guest spoke such excellent English, but the old man's gravity disturbed him.

Gilligan was uncommonly aware of the great responsibility he carried. All civil servants in New Harmony knew of the Harmonizer's personal wish to see Order expand into the Zones of Decadence. In seven years of service, Gilligan had never had so obvious a chance to make his mark as now. Of the thirty-five states of Europe, Berlin was the best candidate. Berlin seemed most decadent of all European states as if, in gaining its freedom with East Germany's drop from the shrinking Soviet orbit, the city had lost its rationale for living. Now, for the first time, a Uni-Eu representative was here to see and listen. Many officials of much higher rank would address the visitor. Nevertheless Gilligan's role was superlatively important—Herr Schmidt's general comfort and well being were in his hands. He could have a striking influence on the impression the German gained during his stay.

Absorbed in such reflections, he shepherded the German through the baggage search. He paced nervously up and down outside the sanitation showers where green disinfectant streams bombarded every traveler. He led Herr Schmidt, now in a fluffy robe, to the cavitation baths where ultrasonic waves exploding under water blasted dirt from every pore. He supervised the louse-spray operation. And finally, he rushed about solicitously to help the Super find his microwaved clothing basket in the irradiation hall.

As they went out into the terminal proper, the German said:

"Are you sure we didn't miss a step in this process, Hank? It seems to me they forgot to pump my stomach."

Gilligan laughed nervously. To distract the German from the absolutely necessary sanitation requirements (after all this was New Harmony, not an underdeveloped nation), he pointed ahead and explained that the gentlemen up front in red jackets, such as the one he wore, were heads of various offices of the Department, and the tall, big man in their center (he didn't want to say "obese") was the Commissioner of Police for Eastcoast. Then, indicating the newsmen and the TV cameras, he expressed the hope that Herr Schmidt might address a few words to the waiting Media.

Schmidt felt both apprehensive and amused as they moved forward. The Eastcoast police officials in their blinding red jackets grinned expectantly as Schmidt approached. They reminded him of salesmen at a convention. All the people in the terminal were neat and tidy to a fault. Despite his rather thorough cleansing, he felt dirty, as if the decadence of Europe still hung about him like a musty odor.

Warm, hamlike hands clasped his, and a huge, gross man bubbled his welcome.

To Gilligan's relief, everything went smoothly. The ComPol did the introductions going from man to man. They were all here, of course, Supply Logistics and Barrier Engineering and Legal and Psychological and all the rest, plus the Regional Crusade Rep and a man from the Lord Mayor's office—in short a VIP reception if Gilligan ever saw one. ComPol even remembered to give Dr. Fieldgreen of Adjustment Education something of a little build up. They'd decided, in laying out the Sales Strategy, to show Schmidt the VPLE test tonight even before his briefings tomorrow. Tonight was the first routine application of the technique.

Then Herr Schmidt spoke briefly to the press, and while Gilligan had hoped for more enthusiasm, at least Herr Schmidt said nothing negative.

ComPol walked them to the helicopter with his arm around Herr Schmidt's shoulder. Herr Schmidt seemed a bit discomfited by that, but then the ComPol couldn't help it; he was a regular glad-handing hugger of a man.

"Now, Karl," the ComPol boomed, "we've got it all laid out for you, old buddy, a little tour, a little nap, dinner, and then a night operation just to get you off to a good start. And all that before your visit officially kicks off tomorrow." He turned to Gilligan. "Now see here, Hank, you make sure Karl here gets whatever he wants. Any old thing! And if you need help, holler. Just give me a ring." He stopped and, still holding Schmidt by the shoulder, he let his arm describe a large circle. "Pretty now, isn't it, Karl. Every last bit of this terminal's new, built after the Flood, and those mosaics are our pride and joy."

The ComPol pointed to the excellent portraits of the Harmonizer all around. Each showed Gunnison in a classic pose—Meditative, Pensive. Executive, Lyric, and Tragic.

Schmidt was a big man, nearly two meters in his stockings, but he felt almost frail next to this giant. He glanced absently at the Harmonizer's five images but his mind lingered with anxiety over the prospect of dinner. The steaks would be five centimeters thick, no doubt, and ComPol would insist that he eat his raw. Ah, these Americans . . .

They went on, and soon they walked in sunshine. Then they crossed macadam and mounted narrow stairs to the copter. Down below ComPol waved an arm.

Inside the airship Gilligan introduced him to the pilot and showed him a good seat. And then, alone at last with Schmidt, he rubbed his hands and said:

"What's your pleasure, Karl? Shall we check you in at the hotel, or shall we take a look-see at good old EC?"

"EC?"

"The Eastcoast Confinement."

"Aha," Schmidt said. "By all means let's look-see good old EC."

Gilligan said: "Let'er rip, Brewster."

The blades began to turn. Moments later they were airborne.

THE scene below reminded Schmidt of a favorite

Gunnison slogan: Let All Things Be Renewed. Whatever had been had been erased by floodwater, bulldozer, or crane. Schmidt saw what he'd already seen in countless newscasts—the prim geometricities of New Harmony. Neat-as-a-pin suburbs rushed by. Shiny red trolleys shimmered up through the foliage. Uniform small cars, all brightly waxed, beaded the highways. Schoolyards teemed with uniformed children (here vacations had been abolished) and shopping arcades with shopping women.

"So," Schmidt said, peering out. "So this is Harmony."

"Impressive, ain't it," Gilligan beamed. "Must look good to you, coming from where you come from."

Schmidt chuckled. "Oh, it's not so bad, Berlin. We struggle on in all our decadence."

"I guess you're right, at that. One gets used to it. Still, if it's anything like it used to be here . . ." Gilligan shook his head. "I remember how it was, Karl. Something else! Filth, pollution, mobs, weirdos! And headlines!? Headlines like you can't believe your eyes! Jesus, how did we ever live?"

"How indeed," Schmidt said with a tiny smile. He kept peering at the scene below.

"I don't know why you folks put up with it over there," Gilligan said. "You don't have to. We don't. We've got the technology if you've got the will. We'll make a deal with you. We'll send the experts, you provide the labor. Anything for a cause."

Schmidt took his eyes off the landscape and turned to Gilligan. "The Clean World Crusade?"

A gleam of enthusiasm brightened Gilligan's eyes. "Yessir! That's the name of the game."

As they approached Manhattan island from the south, Gilligan turned tour guide and explained this and that. Schmidt only half listened. He sought for some sign of the old city, but there was precious little to see. Massive holograph projectors set into the Hudson's banks simulated the ancient skyline, of course, this being tourist season. Gilligan explained how that bit of illusion was generated and at what energy cost. But through the ghostly image of the past, Schmidt saw only squat, uniform buildings. Immediately ahead of them, Gilligan explained, was Eastcoast's administrative center. Schmidt had inferred that. People walked about in the red jackets of Gunnison's civil service. He saw a formation on a roof top. Chanting? Praying? Doing yoga?

Governor's Island passed by on the left. It was still a Coast Guard station but now the service had been renamed. Sea Wall? Beach Sweep? Something like that. The men wore odd, pointed blue caps with yellow pom-poms on top. The Harmonizer took an interest in uniforms and was said to be a crack designer in addition to his many other superlative talents.

They flew over East River and left troubled waters in their wake. Garbage barges on the right moved toward some distant dumping ground much as they'd moved in the old days, but now the barges were painted white and even the garbage had a primly piled look. Then the copter rose to clear the bridges, and Schmidt saw the huge, shimmering bubble of irridescence even before

Gilligan pointed to it with a dramatic gesture.

"There she is, Karl. Beautiful, isn't it. Just *look* at her! Just look at her *shine*!"

The Eastcoast Confinement.

"What you're seeing there," Gilligan explained, "is a dynaletonic laminar flow of lectromag radiation. Ozonified, too. Only its not just one laminate but about fifteen hundred plies, like. It's about four meters thick at the bottom, but it thins out on top. We generate it in a Lunac converter. Darn expensive, energy-wise. Sixty thousand kilo-cals per square meter of surface."

To the fifty-nine year old eyes of a policeman it was just a shimmering bubble, an extremely large bubble. It began around Forty-Second Street (if there was still such a thing) and extended away to the north as far as the eye could see. A blue-gray haze above it suggested smoke.

Passage through the barrier wasn't lethal, Gilligan said, but it caused temporary paralysis and extreme nausea followed by migraine. The field's strength increased geometrically with each breaching, and mass exodus from the Confinement was practically impossible.

Schmidt nodded. He understood all this, and Gilligan's explanation was superfluous. He wondered what went on inside. The human aspect interested him far more than the whizz-bang stuff. Americans knew and loved whizz-bang. But did they understand the sociology?

They made toward the bubble, approaching it fast. On the left Schmidt saw midtown Manhattan, the transformed Manhattan. He could see into the straight, uniform streets and inspect the low concrete buildings, each exactly the same as the other. The monotony was relieved only by large billboards. The people in the streets, however, were reassuringly people—women chatted in doorways and little children ran and bicycled about.

Then they left the city behind and flew parallel to the barrier for a while. At one point the ship began to vibrate and the copter veered to the left.

"Neutralizer," Gilligan said. "Brewster just turned it on."

They moved through. For a second, but only for a second, Schmidt felt a surge of nausea and pain at his temples.

THE Eastcoast Confinement could be divided fairly neatly into four quadrants. This was not a physical division, purely, although it was also that, complete with walls, towers, water or rubble-filled trenches, and all the rest. Rather, it arose from the tribal patterns within the reservation. In the east where the helicopter entered, Peacefreak held sway—and a bloodthirsty bunch they were too, Gilligan said. They faced the Maoling redcaps on the west and adjoined Ecofreak to the south. Panthermess had its domains on the north, but Gilligan explained that Panther "fingers' extended well into the other territories. The Panthers were much in demand for the medical services they provided. Each tribe was further subdivided into so-called "packs," and each pack had its own "turf" and took part in the foodwar in a kind of rotation, like.

Gilligan wondered what else Schmidt needed to know by way of context when the German asked him curtly why none of this was in the literature he'd been sent. Gilligan replied that it was all of marginal interest compared with the technology. He worried a little because Herr Schmidt had begun to frown in an odd sort of way, and so Gilligan hastened to assure him that very ample sociological data were available and would be provided in the course of briefings tomorrow afternoon.

Schmidt frowned because he was thinking. Here it was. His oldest arguments with the Senate came back to him now. He had argued with the gentlemen politicians. He had told them what he had suspected—namely that inside the Confinements lived societies as legitimate and real as those outside. He had never been able to buy the NPSO propaganda to the effect that the people Inside were the dregs of the earth, incompetents, incapables, antisocials, degenerates—people, in other words, whose presence in the larger society represented a danger to the whole. He knew it couldn't be that simple. He had cited the facts of life to the Senate. Even penitentiaries were organized into societies. What Gilligan had told him, and what he now saw, convinced him that he had been right.

Down below he saw a part of old New York—a jumble of buildings high and low, canyons and valleys and open spaces, real brick, cement, steel, and glass rather than holographic images. It should have looked like a grim urban desert, but it wasn't quite that. Everywhere he saw green, green of every conceivable shade—the dark green of bushes, the light green of new sprouts, the variable green of carrot tops, cabbages, lettuce, turnips, and other plants he didn't recognize. It seemed as if old Manhattan had been overgrown with vegetation. It greened on rooftops, streets, squares, yards, windowsills.

Next he was struck by the mass of people. He saw them everywhere. They swarmed down there in clumps and bunches. They sat darkly. They worked in rows amidst the green. Faces turned up toward them and hands waved. Schmidt imagined that he saw the people smile, but he couldn't be sure of that. They flew too high and a blue haze from a thousand chimneys obscured the view.

They moved over a mile-long, snaking queue and Gilligan pointed to it.

"That's a food line down there, a pack distribution point. And that over there, that clump of men with axes? See the red hats? Maoling slaves tearing up the pavement to make more strip farms. They cultivate every bit of land they can find."

"Maoling *slaves*?"

"Yep. That's the latest. In the last couple of months Peacefreak has started taking slaves, and our guess is it's spreading all over the Confinement. They work 'em twenty hours a day on half rations. Keeps the population down." Gilligan chuckled.

"Your food shipments . . . ?"

"Not enough; not nearly enough." Gilligan chuckled again. "Let's face it, Karl. We're not trying very hard to keep 'em alive in here; but they fight back."

Schmidt meant to follow up on that remark, but his attention snagged on a weird, impressive structure that now detached itself from the haze. It was

a dome topped by three slender needles of un-
equal length. The building stood in a large square
of cleared ground. Masses of people filled the
square with a dark dotting of heads. The structure
seemed made of bits and pieces of waste
material—glass, brick, steel, and plastic all
welded together in a loose reticulation. The massive construct gleamed in the mixed light of afternoon sunshine and shimmering barrier. This was
certainly not old New York, nor was it New Harmony. This was something new and somehow
alien, the expression of some kind of spirit;
Schmidt sensed a kind of grandeur and defiance
in this aggregation of materials.

He pointed to it. "And that?"

"That's Sophia Grande." The tone dismissed
the whole thing in such a way that Schmidt, already alerted, grew suspicious.

"What is it? A church?"

"Our Lady of the Expansion."

"That wasn't in my briefing package either.
What is this? Some sort of recent development?"

Gilligan shook his head and curled his lips in
an expression of contempt. "Naw, not really. The
structure is fairly new, but the myth is almost as
old as the Confinement. They say down there that
the barrier will come down some day and the
people inside will inherit the earth. They say a
woman will lead them, so they built her a
church." The voice expressed scorn, and Schmidt
had a momentary glimpse of a slightly different
Richard H. Gilligan. Gilligan the hard-nosed cop.
For a second there was silence filled only by the
chopping whirr of blades. "Fat chance," Gilligan
said. "Cold day in hell. We've got this barrier on a

'usion plant, and that, believe me, ain't gonna run
out of fuel." Silence. "Brewster, you better get up
a bit. They're bound to take a shot at us." Turning
to Schmidt, he pointed down. "See that double
wall and the water trench? That's the border be-
ween Peacefreak and Maoling. There. Those dark
half circles? Catapult nests."

A religious myth strong enough to engender a
public works built by a mass of people under
some kind of tight coordination would mean the
presence of real culture down below, something
that these dregs of humanity were not supposed to
possess. Schmidt set that aside for the moment
and concentrated on the scene.

Near the catapult nests half-naked men worked
feverishly. In seconds fire-darts rose up toward
them reaching for the copter's bottom-mounted
fuel tanks. But Brewster had lifted the ship in a
right-leaning circle and the darts fell short. The
ship passed almost directly over Sophia Grande
as it turned, and Schmidt got a better look at the
shining needles of the construct. There was something odd about the light reflection and the
geometry of the panels laid on the needles' surface. What had seemed like panes of glass to
Schmidt from a greater distance now resembled
panels of some kind. Solar panels? But that, of
course, was ludicrous. The technology was denied to these miserable inhabitants of this incred-
ible, green ghetto. More likely small hothouses
used to grow food.

"How many people live in here?" he asked. The
Eastcoast Confinement looked far larger than he'd
imagined from the literature.

"Eight million, give or take, we—"

"Excuse me, Hank; did you say eight million
The literature—"

"I know, Karl. The official statistics only lis
principals, and there are only two million princi
pals down there."

"Principals?"

"I don't want to anticipate your briefings, Karl
but here goes anyway." Gilligan's tone turned
tutorial. "Crime is a social phenomenon, not an
individual thing. When the Mind embraces
crime, it pollutes or infects all those who co
vibrate with it."

Gilligan turned to Schmidt to see if the German
followed him. This was deep stuff, and Europeans
were terribly skeptical. That's why the World
Crusade made so little progress in the Zones of
Decadence. But the German seemed receptive
and Gilligan went on:

"When someone commits a crime, we obviously find the co-vibrators, too, and in they go, the
whole lot."

"I take it, then," Schmidt said, "that 'co-
vibrators' are . . . what? Husbands, wives, children?"

Gilligan nodded. "That's right, Karl. That's
why we have eight million down here, although
the exact number isn't known. Eight million's a
guesstimate. The input is down to a few thousand
a year, and they kill that many in the foodwar and
the tribal raids. On the other hand, the birth rate
. . ." Gilligan pointed to the copter's padded
stitched ceiling and shook his head. "You'd swear
they're *deliberately* breeding. Goes to show you
that they're antisocial. It's suicide to breed in a
confinement, social suicide." A thought made

him smile. "Gunnison says we might have to import people from the Confinement one of these days. Anti-fer is working too well on our side. Population on the Outside is down to a hundred and fifty million, but counting all of our Confinements, all forty-seven of them, the Inside population's pushing sixty and it's growing."

In the silence Schmidt pondered that relationship. The birthrate was up? In all other industrial nations, it was dropping at an alarming rate.

"Say, Karl, why not!" Gilligan cried suddenly. "Let's just do it right now. The official tour isn't till Friday, but you might as well get a look at the best population control device ever invented—and the oldest." He chuckled. "Brewster, let's circle by the Pile for just a sec, and then you'd better head out again."

THE words "foodwar" and "pile" did not appear in the literature, but Schmidt understood the reference. The population was supplied by helicopters equipped with neutralizers such as this one had. Schmidt expected a large mob scene at points where the food was distributed . . . people trampling each other. But when they came upon the scene, he saw with the cold horror of a man who'd seen many things that it was worse than that. This was a real war.

Long before they reached the spot. Schmidt saw the busy movement of large transports far away behind the haze of smoke. They came in from the Jersey side in an endless line. Huge bales swung by cables from the bottom. The ships dipped, released the bales, rose up high again, and headed back.

The locus of the deposition was a large square surrounded by old brownstones. In an area five blocks square the ubiquitous green of the Confinement was conspicuous by absence. The copters came in and released bales in the center of the square, and it was indeed a huge pile of materials. In a circle all around it, defending the mouths of street radiants, men fought a fierce battle against attacking masses—but it wasn't a mob against a mob so much as organized military formations against organized defenders shielded from rooftop arrow fire and wheeled catapult darts by barriers built of broken crates, sacks of sand, and concrete rubble.

Brewster brought the ship to a hover, and they watched the fight. Below them a long line of women and children marched southeast in single file. They carried crates on back, head, and slung on bicycles. Schmidt was reminded of ants.

"Peacefreaks again," Gilligan said in a tone of displeasure. "They dominate the distribution. Peacefreaks, see? You can tell by the yellow band they've got tied around their arms and the yellow shirts some of 'em wear. If we were closer you could see the symbol. That's the Hundred and Twelfth Street Pack. Our records show that Peacies are in charge here sixty-four point two percent of the time. And they only have thirty-three point nine percent of the population."

"Are you sure it's point nine?" Schmidt asked.

"Absolutely," Gilligan said. "You'll see, Karl. We've got this technology down pat. Every transport brings back a report, and it goes right into a computer. We know all about these birds. Stats,

everything. Nothing you have to invent for your-
selves in Berlin. We'll come in and set it up for
you free of charge. And we'll guarantee that it'll
work."

"I'm sure it will, Hank," Schmidt said.

Gilligan looked at the German. He heard something in the man's voice. But the long face was
serious, and the gray eyes were fixed steadily at
the scene below.

"Nose down a bit, Brewster. Herr Schmidt
might want to see the symbol."

"There's no need for that," Schmidt said. "Does
it go on like this all the time?" He watched a
salient of men in red railroader caps. They had
stormed over the bodies of their dead and had cut
and slashed their way past the barrier to a corner
of the Pile. Immediately a column of women
materialized in the feeder street, and men began
to throw bales and sacks across the barrier.

"Twenty-four hours a day," Gilligan answered.
"Not on the Sabbath, of course. We don't deliver
on the Sabbath." Gilligan shook his head. He
watched the battle with a professional eye.
"Peacefreak's too strong," he said. "He turned to
Schmidt." You're just in time to see us try a little
innovation tonight. ComPol mentioned it to you.
What we call an adjustment operation. Peacefreak's too strong and must be weakened, or else
we'll get unification down there, and that's
dangerous."

"Why so?"

"They've got some awfully smart people in
there. Physicists, chemists, people like that.
Brainy folks are often antisocial. They could in-

vent a neutralizer in no time at all. But they can't
massproduce'em—not so long as they keep fighting. So we keep'em off balance."

"What'll you do, exactly, tonight?"

"Peacefreak's too well led," Gilligan said.
"That's why they keep gaining turf. We'll pick up
some of their chiefs on girly raid and . . ." Gilligan hesitated, looking for the word. "Let's say we
give them a bit of education—that's permitted by
the Constitution. Our stats people say four chiefs
should do it. Peacefreak will drop down to around
thirty percent or so."

"In population?"

"No." Gilligan gestured toward the battle. "In
RD."

"In RD?"

"Resource Dominance. Control of the pile."

They watched in silence as the redcapped men
were dislodged again by the furiously slashing
counterattack of blood-drenched Peacefreaks.

Gilligan gestured. "Maoling can't do it. They're
too weak and starving too fast for OPMB."

The initials were multiplying. "OPMB?"

"Optimum Population Mass Balance," Gilligan
said. "You'll get all that in the briefing tomorrow.
Have you seen enough?"

Schmidt nodded. Involuntarily he thought of a
rat trap he had once seen. It'd been a box with a
trap door. The rats fell down into the box and were
slowly starved into cannibalism. As the copter
rose and turned again, this time to the south, he
made a note to ask about "girly raids" and to
inquire how it was that "education" was "permitted" by the Constitution, and how much "education" would weaken the leadership abilities of

Peacefreak tribal chiefs. But for the moment he didn't want to pursue the matter. He was tired. His internal body-clock told him it was eleven at night, although here the sun still shot oblique rays into the smoky atmosphere beneath the barrier.

II

EMMANUEL Toronto Salazar Smith. Or Emmanuel Smith. Or Manny, for short.

Manny stared at the gorgeous three-color graffiti painted on the bathroom wall above the toilet that no longer worked and had never worked and wouldn't be allowed to work even if it did—the fecal matter was too precious to waste. What you didn't put on the crops you burned as fuel. The graffiti was a bold yellow swirl faintly resembling an E and a double S. A red border enclosed the letters, and two fat green dots hung over the rumplike curve of the last letter on the right. They called those dots the eyes of Emmanuel Toronto Salazar Smith. Or Manny, for short. Everyone knew Manny-Man in the tenblock turf where that symbol and those eyes warned interlopers to stay off Brinco territory.

He shifted his eyes from wall to mirror to help clumsy hands tie the bright yellow tie under the collar of a starched white shirt. A neat suit jacket hung from the rusty hook of a shower-curtain rod. Manny flicked a bit of dust from its arm and then put it on. Neat and tidy. You had to be spotless out there or the squeeze would nail you before you even saw the chickie line. He had worn his raiding suit four times in his life, and this was the fifth time. It brought back memories of pain and a kind of fear that he never felt inside the Realm. It was the fear of his cells, the fear of his blood, the fear of his guts, the fear not of Manny-Man but of that which Manny-Man carried about with him, his bod. The fear was already beginning. It would grow slowly on the way to the chapel. It would grow greater and greater with every step of that endless walk south to the border. And finally it would be there screaming in his brain when he'd face the Fire. That's why he had delayed so long. But now the time had finally come. He couldn't stay Manny-Man much longer without a Queen. His eyes would be put out, covered over, and the Pack would sell him off to Maoling as a common slave.

He pulled the jacket down and pulled in his chin. Almost. He looked almost puritan. The face was a bit too Latin—dark and swarthy despite the camouflaging powder. They said that browns and blacks lived out there, and they did, but Manny knew and they all knew inside the Realm that browns and blacks didn't belong in Harmony. Slowly they brought them all in here and shoved them in through the barrier locks, with the locks set at full force, so you'd get a good feel of what it was like, crossing the Fire. Manny didn't mind so much with the young men and women. It did them good to know what it was all about. But it hurt with the oldies and the children who rolled around on the ground twitching and spasming and throwing up the precious food they'd brought in with them in their stomachs.

He turned and swept the gold into his hand from the empty water tank of the useless toilet. He stared at the pendant for a second then put the whole mess into his pocket. He was ready to go.

In the Big Room lounging rubes looked up from chores. They were busy with whetstones sharpening swords or tipping arrows or dipping darts into steaming asphalt reclaimed from pavements lifted up to make more farms. They broke into derisive laughter and pointed fingers at him. They made noises in the cheeks and called him Neaty-toe and Sensy-wensy. But Manny sensed their approval now. There was a joy and glee in their abandoned yelping. They saw him dressed and they were reassured. He half suppressed a smile and gave them the thumb. At the door he turned.

"Tonight," he called. He fixed them with dark, brooding eyes whose whites were almost dark yellow and were marked by fine red arteries. They rested swords, darts, and arrows and settled down to listen. "Tonight we'll have a Queen."

Manny ran down stairs. The rube cheer resounded behind him and echoed dully through the bare brick halls of the ancient building.

He walked through dark streets eyeing the walls. Competing graffiti had mushroomed here and there in the last day or so. His rubes had claimed they couldn't stop it. He suspected that some of them had painted signs, eager to be pack chief themselves. "You lost your stroke. Your

queen's fled. You got no gripe, Manny-Boy."
Manny-Boy, the rubes had said. Not Manny-Man.

Folk lined the sidewalks three deep getting a
breath of night air. Eyes followed him and heads
nodded in approval. They saw his raiding dress
and they knew that he was Manny-Man again now
that he'd resolved to take the Ordeal and do it
again—go up against the Man's wall for a Queen.
Back in charge . . . *if* he came back.

Manny didn't know how it had all started, the
business with the queens. It lay very far back,
several years, and in the Realm you lived one day
at a time. Suddenly they were there. One pack had
one and then another. Packs with queens did better in the war. The Virgin Mom had foretold this
long, long ago, back when they were still building
the engines and you could still go out of the Realm
by subway. And then it was like this. You *had* to
have a queen. The people demanded it. And the
only real queen was one you took from a chickie
line. They waited for you. They had precious
things hidden away in their clothing and on their
body . . . things that the squeeze would catch at
the official gates with detectors. The people said
those precious things guarded the pack luck.
Manny-Man had his doubts about that, but you
never knew, and without the queen the rubes led
poorly and the boys didn't fight.

He headed for the Brinco chapel aware that
women detached themselves from the crowd and
came in his wake like an ever-growing comet's
tail. He saw it up ahead, the gleaming chapel, still
only half finished. One spire of burning steel-
glass-stone reached up above the dark, surrounding tenements. Four holy panels from Sophia

Grande had been installed already to make power
in the chapel's basement. They had lathes and
drills and other machinery down there that the
queens had told him to assemble. It was holy work
indeed. One year, two years? The work moved
forward slowly, but the time would come some
wondrous night when neutralizers would open
up the barrier in a thousand places and the folk
would burst from the Confinement and rage over
the land like a herd of hungry locusts following
Her lead.

He stopped for a second and looked at the
construction—a wondrous design he'd made himself, modeled on the Grande. When it was done,
the Lady would smile on Brinco. No other pack in
Peacefreak would have a chapel so beautiful.
Someday they'd call it Emmanuel Toronto
Salazar Smith's gift to Her of the Expansion.

He entered the chapel and kissed the stone
book's nipple by the door. "Mercy please," he
murmured. Head inclined he walked toward the
empty wood-cage suspended from the loft above
the votive light extinguished now that no queen
sat and prophesied from the cage. He knelt down,
careful not to smudge the raiding suit.

Slowly he let the feeling rise in him.

It came readily enough. He felt longing and
desire. The holy bed stood on the right. Four
weeks had passed since she'd been here. He let the
feeling expand from the particularities of that one
girl into the universaility of the Lady. Emotions
choked him, and the feeling burst out in a sob.

"Queen Mother," he cried with lifted head
sensing the people in the darkness behind him,
feeling their emotion of dread at the agony in his

voice. "Queen mother, precious bride and crone."

His voice rang clear with erotic ardor. It shivered him to say it.

"You saw fit to leave out midst as a slave to Maoling."

"Maoling," the women murmured in the back. The murmur grated with harsh anger. Yes. They looked at the right altar railing ruined in the last assault when a handful of rubes and men had died in that surprise raid weeks ago. Manny had been at the Pile with most of the men. The redcaps had ravished her away.

"Queen Mother Bride!"

His eyes filled with tears of longing. Emmanuel Toronto Salazar Smith had loved Betty Simple, Brinco's queen. He'd dreaded the time when she would leave him in the course of things to journey to Sophia Grande. But she'd been taken before her year was up. He sobbed. He almost saw her pouting in the cage. She always pouted and her oracles were mixed with dark obscenities. But she had clung to him always in sacred intercourse on Janenights when the people came with candles. He saw her lay on the holy bed raised high on carved stilts below the cage. She had a yellow bow tied in her hair and peace signs painted on her naked thighs.

"Queen of Expansion, give my heart strength," he sobbed. "Secure me in the fire of the wall. Make me invisible to the squeeze. Grant me a queen for Brinco whose lips shall call the future clear. Mercy thanks."

"Mercy thanks," the women whispered, and it sounded like wind passing over straw.

Manny bent his head.

Slowly a lone voice behind him too up the
Hymn in reedy tones. Then they all came in, a
hundred Brinco fem-folk voices. The sound grew
and enveloped him.

Lady High in gracious splendour
Grant us now the land beyond.
Homage to you now we render
To secure the Sacred Bond.
Jee, jee, jimeny high,
Jee, jee, jimeny low.
To secure the Sacred Bond
To secure the Sacred Bow . . .

MANNY-MAN Toronto Salazar Smith rose, turned,
and passed out between the women. Their dark
eyes rested on his powdered face in serious, ques-
tioning expectation. At the door a deaconess gave
him the wooden flower painted white and affixed
to the end of a carved stick. Four times he'd held
the stick; this was the fifth time. It would secure
his passage through friendly and hostile territories despite the puritan threads and the yellow
tie.

Soon he left behind the last of the yellow-red
graffities with the green eyes of Manny-Man. He
marched with fixed gaze, flower stick held high.
The people made way for him and murmured
"Mercy thanks." Then later he entered Ecofreak
land and they said nothing at all but let him go
from pack turf to pack turf toward Forty-Second
Street where lately Eco's had breached another
wall and let raiders use the gap for a decagram of
gold. The gold was in his pocket. Five rings, two
armbands, forty-five teeth, and a pendant. He

wasn't sure about the pendant. That might be amalgam.

Security tightened around Forty-Fifth Street. Ecofreaks knew they had a good thing. This was supposed to be one of the best gates through the Fire, a low-pressure spot in the shield. (They all claimed that, of course, they all did, and it was never true.) This pack had no need to fight on the Pile every eighteen days. Not when you had a gate. They had the gold and bought the bread. Checkpoint followed checkpoint. Each had a little scale and he had to empty his pocket. Each time a shrewd man fingered the pendant.

"That's amalgam."

"It may be that, but I'm a gram over."

"So you are, Peacy, so you are."

They examined the seal on the bottom of the flower-stick pressed there by the Virgin Mom of Sophia Grande with a ring on melted polyethylene. Then they waved him on. These men said "Mercy thanks." For them it was a business. They didn't take sides.

At the last stop they took his wealth and gave him directions.

"Down into the sub over there, three flights. Then you go along the rails to the right for eighty meters, give or take. And then you'll see a cave-in on your left with a narrow break to the left of that. Through there. In a bit you'll see the shimmer. Good raiding."

To them it was all routine.

"How much for a torch?"

"Four nails."

"Jeez. You rubes know how to squeeze."

The men shrugged.

Manny-Man gave up four precious cigarettes and they lit a torch for him from one struck in a crack in the wall.

Emmanuel Toronto Salazar Smith set out with a torch in one hand and a flower in the other down dark stairs to get a queen for Brinco Pack lest the Lady frown and the pack fail in battle on the Pile. In a way he held their future in his hand.

THE dinner in Karl Schmidt's honor was drawing to an end. Servants served ice cream to the guests who sat in bright red jackets around the oval table in a private dining room of the Crusade House. On the walls hung tapestries with slogans.

The Special Assistant to the Lord Mayor had the word.

"Herr Schmidt," he said, "you ask about the philosophical basis of the Confinement. Let me put it like this. The basis is mercy and freedom. The guidance laid out in the Harmonizer's Science of Morals is clear. He writes, 'And make no mistakes about it. Punishment is presumption, but nonviolent withdrawal is permitted.'"

The Lord Mayor said: "That's a mouthful."

The youthful Regional Crusade Rep broke in eagerly: "What Hendricks is saying, Herr Schmidt—"

"What I'm saying," Hendricks asserted, "is that we have eliminated punishment. It no longer exists."

The Lord Mayor: "It's gone, it's gone."

The City's Secretary for Perpetual Harmony leaned over his ice cream dish and gestured with an index finger: "The Constitution expressly forbids punishment, and we abide by that."

"But we have a Cosmic Right to live in Harmony," Hendricks augmented.

The Lord Mayor: "There you have it."

Hendricks:" We may withdraw nonviolently."

The secretary: "And we've done so, in effect."

The Rep: "While we allow the dissidents every freedom within the boundaries of the Confinement."

"They live in bliss with their co-vibrators," Schmidt said.

"All have the same rights, of course. Principals and co-vibrators. We make no distinctions whatever."

The Lord Mayor shook his head: "None! None!"

Hendricks continued: "They have their lives, and we have ours, and that's the Lesser Harmony."

"And the Greater?"

"That'll come in time. We have a program we call Gradual Life Support Cutback."

"GLSC," the Rep threw in.

"Which is being implemented as their indigenous agriculture improves. Ultimately—"

"Pardon me, Mr. Hendricks, but do you honestly expect eight million people to live off agriculture on a part of Manhattan?"

"We don't play numbers games around here, Herr Schmidt," Hendricks replied. "Eight million, two million, a hundred thousand. As the Harmonizer has so aptly written, 'All things reach their appointed level.' "

Schmidt said: "With all due respect, Mr. Hendricks, but back home we'd call that genocide."

The Secretary for Perpetual Harmony broke the brief, awkward silence: "Herr Schmidt, GLSC relies on *gradual* adjustments, natural attrition. We expect the birthrate to drop inside."

"But now it's rising."

"A temporary phenomenon, Herr Schmidt."

The Lord Mayor nodded: "Temporary, temporary."

The Regional Rep explained: "We believe that the rate of growth shows signs of declining. Our experts on population dynamics expect that once a certain point is reached, the birthrate will take a sharp dip."

"It seems to me that point should've been reached long ago."

The Secretary shook his head: "Under normal circumstances, maybe. But these are antisocials."

"Antisocials and their co-vibrators, don't forget," Schmidt said.

"Yes, of course."

"Look here, you guys!" The booming voice was the ComPol's. He had been silent too long. "Karl, here, he's a practical man. Let's not bend his ear with philosophy and stuff like that. The Confinement *works*. That's where I come out on this. Hey, Karl, how about a little steak sauce. The rest of us are on ice cream, and you haven't even touched your steak."

Schmidt waved a hand defensively. "My stomach is still in Berlin."

"Hey, that's a good one," ComPol chuckled. "His stomach's in Berlin. Karl, that's what I like about you, your sense of humor. Say, you won't mind watching tonight's operation, will you? Time change, and all that?"

"You've convinced me that it will be interesting."

The Rep broke in eagerly: "We finally think we've solved a big problem, Herr Schmidt. The Commissioner has said it well. The Confinement *works*, but—"

Hendricks cut in: "But that doesn't mean that we don't have very real practical problems."

The Lord Mayor: "Very real."

"For example?"

The Secretary took a turn to elaborate: "I think that all of these gentlemen would agree that there remains a significant danger from within."

"From within the Confinement?"

"Yes."

"The Ghengis Khan threat."

The Rep began: "What Mr. Hendricks means—"

"I mean the danger of unification."

The Lord Mayor nodded gravely: "Ghengis Khan, yes!"

ComPol took the floor: "You've got to see it like this, Karl. There's a lot of real smart alecks in there, too smart for their own good."

Schmidt said: "I believe Gilligan mentioned that to me. He fears that neutralizers might be invented and—"

"Hell, we assume they've done that," ComPol said. "We're worried about mass production. They might start that if they ever unify under some Ghengis Khan."

Hendricks took the lead: "In practical terms, Herr Schmidt, we're limited in what we can do. The Constitution is clear on the subject, and so are the Harmonizer's writings. We may withdraw nonviolently, but we can't meddle with their internal politics."

The Lord Mayor said: "No. That would be

wrong, that's for sure."

Schmidt looked around and addressed them all: "Isn't that a little incongruous? You lock up a third of the population but you scrupulously avoid interference on some Constitutional basis."

"Herr Schmidt." Once more the Secretary filled a silence. "I think all of us would object to the phrase 'lock up.' Sequestration is the term we use, and it is far more descriptive. 'Locking up' implies a form of punishment. We don't punish in New Harmony. You might, in Berlin, but we don't deprive people of their Freedom. We merely sequester them into their vibrational community."

The Rep came in eagerly: "The writings are quite explicit on the subject. Why, in Moral Science the Harmonizer writes—"

"Farley," Hendricks broke in, "Herr Schmidt is not all that interested in the writings, I'm sure. But now that you bring it up, the quote you're groping for is: 'The just seek justice and the base baseness. Let us therefore establish a place of justice and a place of baseness, and let Mind itself sequester the wheat from the chaff.' "

The Lord Mayor agreed: "Well put, well put."

"Nevertheless, you do want to interfere."

"We merely want to ensure that the Sequestration remains effective."

"Why don't you let Mind do that?"

The Rep eagerly threw in: "The Harmonizer writes: 'Mind works through Man as Man works through Mind.' "

"So you have to give Mind a Hand?"

The Secretary for Perpetual Harmony smiled painfully and said: "I see, Herr Schmidt, that your sense of humor is very active, indeed. You sense a contradiction here, but the conflict is more apparent than real. Precisely put, the doctrine goes something like this: The 'hand' you refer to is actually a manifestation of Mind. Farley's quote should be understood in its poetic, not in its metaphysical sense. It appears in the Harmonizer's Science of Aesthetics.''

COMPOL HAD grown restless again: "As one practical man to another, Karl, let me say this. We're lucky as hell that the boys in there go on girly raids regular as clockwork, or we'd have our work cut out for us.''

"Tell me about that. The phrase intrigued me when Gilligan used it this afternoon.''

"Girly raid?''

"Yes.''

"Well, it's like this, Karl. When you're dealing with weirdos and crazies, there's always something like that—something you can't explain, and the girly raids are one of those things. The big studs in there, the chiefs, they have to kidnap their girls from the Outside. It's a kind of . . . of a . . . an act of what-you-ma-call it . . . machismo, like. I mean, those guys go through agonies coming and going, and I guess it makes them look pretty big in the eyes of the crowd inside.''

The Rep interjected: "Of course, there is a more sophisticated explanation—''

"Which is,'' Hendricks continued, "that there's a differential moral pressure on this side of the barrier that pulls the chiefs. As it says in the Science of Morals, 'The Victim is by far the stronger in such cases, acting like a magnet on filings.' ''

The Lord Mayor "Apt, apt."

The Secretary said. pointing with a spoon: "I see that you're puzzled, Herr Schmidt. What Hendricks means is that—"

"I was coming to that," Hendricks said. "The theory is simply that we have a certain number of unidentified co-vibrators out here who attract the chiefs."

"Let me see if I understand you," Schmidt said. "You're saying that the girls—some girls—wish to be kidnapped and so—"

"That's evident—"

"—they get what they deserve?"

"Where *I* come out on this," the ComPol said, reasserting the practical again, "is that they come; and that gives us a chance to educate them."

"Gilligan mentioned that. What do you do? Use some kind of drug?"

"Goodness no," the Rep cried.

The Secretary was also shocked: "That would be clearly illegal."

Hendricks: "A breach of the Constitution."

The Lord Mayor: "Breach, that's the word."

ComPol said: "Karl, let me tell you what we'll be doing tonight and in the future. We'll vipple the guys and send them back in."

"'Vipple' stands for Victim-Perpetrator Life Exchange," Hendricks explained.

The Rep chimed in with: "It's an educational tool, pure and simple."

"It ain't simple!" ComPol protested. "It takes up three floors of a good-sized building. And it's damned expensive, too. But it should work. The boys tell me it'll work. It's like this, Karl. Used to be, we lectured to the chiefs. For one day. That's all we're allowed. We used to lecture them till they were blue in the face. But that didn't work. Now with vipple, we've got'em.''

The Secretary held up his hands. "Gentlemen, gentlemen. You're going too fast for Herr Schmidt. He looks from face to face and I see that he is confused. Let me explain, Herr Schmidt. VPLE is a new discovery, a phenomenal new device invented in our penal laboratories by Dr. Fieldgreen.''

ComPol: "You met him this afternoon."

And the Rep: "It's a consciousness expander."

Then Hendricks: "Let Herb explain."

"What it does, Herr Schmidt, is this. It transfers the experience of one person to another, and vice-versa. Clearly you get a tremendous expansion of consciousness."

"That's possible?"

"We've done it!"

ComPol added: "Works like gangbusters."

The Rep exulted: "It's a real breakthrough."

Schmidt shook his head. "I don't see how that would serve your purposes. How will that incapacitate the chiefs? That's your object, isn't it? To destroy their effectiveness?"

Hendricks pushed his ice cream dish aside and said: "Whatever makes a chief a chief in there, it must be his superb adaptation, right?"

"All right," Schmidt said. "I would agree."

"Adaptation's a state of mind, right?"

Schmidt shrugged. "All right; go on."

"With VPLE, we expand the guy's consciousness. That *changes* his state of mind."

"Right," Schmidt conceded, "but it doesn't follow that he'll be maladapted. More likely, he'll be better adapted."

"Not so," Hendricks said.

"He loses his charisma," the Rep interjected, "and that's what these boys rule by, in there."

"They become much more 'reflective'—that's the phrase." This was the Secretary.

"We've got proof in the case of Abe Herzenberg Sultzy Chico Kid."

The Lord Mayor nodded: "Yes, the Kid."

"Abe Herzenberg . . . ?"

ComPol saw his opening. "We've only vippled one guy so far. Abe Herzenberg Sultzy Chico Kid. (All of these guys have these long names—more machismo.) We knew it's work from the animal experiments, but we had to have a test case—for the legality of it. So we vippled the Kid, and then we had some friends of ours file a friendly suit."

The Rep: "It went all the way to the Celestial Arbiters."

Hendricks: "And the case held. VPLE is a legal educational tool."

The Lord Mayor: "Legal's the word."

"But what I wanted to say, Karl, is that it worked on this Sultzy Kid. Afterwards he was kind of a zombie, like, and so was the victim.

For a second there was silence. Then Schmidt began: "So you have a new technical innovation that, in effect . . ." He stopped. Richard H. Gilligan had appeared at the door of the dining room. "It appears, gentlemen, that my guide is ready to take me from your midst."

Heads turned. Then Hendricks said: "Herr Schmidt. Let me try to sum up the Lord Mayor's thoughts about your visit. The people of Berlin and the people of the United Harmonies have a long and friendly history of mutual cooperation. We'd like your city to be the first on the Continent to try a confinement. Conditions warrant it. Your people want it. Your Senate would vote for it if only you withdraw your opposition. The Mayor has that assurance from the delegation that came to visit us last year. The time for action is now, and we are at your service."

The Lord Mayor said: "My sentiments, my sentiments."

The Regional Rep: "Such a venture would cement our deep cultural ties."

And the ComPol: "Karl, old buddy, believe me, it's good to know they're behind that barrier, all nicely sequestered up, the whole damned lot of them, safe and secure."

Finally, the Secretary for Perpetual Harmony: "A toast, gentlemen. I give you the Berlin Confinement."

Schmidt gave his glass of carrot juice a tiny lift. But he didn't drink to what he judged was pious, ignorant, official genocide, no, not even to be polite.

THEY drove out of the Eastcoast Police Compound over a ribbed metal surface that made talk difficult in a vehicle Gilligan had called a van but Schmidt would have described as a station wagon. He sat in front between Gilligan and a uniformed chauffeur.

It was nighttime in Manhattan.

Schmidt found it odd to drive through what seemed to him more like a military reservation than a city (with its low concrete buildings, virtually empty streets, and its "buttoned-up-tight-for-the-night" atmosphere) while all around flickered a luminous replica of old New York. Sometimes the streets projected by the holograph generators didn't coincide with the real, the new, the neo-puritan road, so that the van drove through buildings, statues, lamp posts.

When they got off the ribbed street and the high-pitched hum stopped, Gilligan began to describe the operation that lay ahead, but Schmidt only half listened. His mind still mulled over the dinner conversation.

Gilligan said that catching a chief was relatively easy once you knew the exit points he used. The barrier could be crossed at any point, of course, but the chiefs always came out underground to avoid detection. The surface was constantly patroled, and it was easy to pick them up as they spasmed on the ground. It took the better part of half an hour to recover from passage, and the chiefs liked to do so in privacy, of course. Now up ahead was an underground breach the Peace-freaks liked to use because it was near the territory, and that's where they were going now. The Department had set up an observation room from which the breach could be watched through hidden cameras. Once a chief was spotted, detectives would follow him until he made his move against a girl. Then they'd hustle him off to be vippled.

Gilligan asked Schmidt if he had been told about VPLE, and the German said yes, he'd been told a little something. Gilligan then launched off into a description of that. He knew a lot about the animal tests that had been conducted and the technology—work, he said, that had grown out of experiments with brain wave control in the sixties and seventies. But when Gilligan noticed that Schmidt was pensive, he stopped, and they rode on in silence.

Schmidt thought about RD, OPMB, GLSC, VPLE. His detailed briefing package had made no mention of these things. Nor had there been mention of complex social arrangements inside the Confinements. No. Nor mention of a religious movement that had thrown up a truly intriguing, original building. Despite its humble materials and seemingly random construction, Sophie Grande (even the name had stuck), reminded him in an odd sort of way of the cathedral in Cologne. Our Lady of the Expansion. It darkened his mood to think about that. Was it possible that an authentic new religion had been born inside the Confinement—a new inspiration that would die along with the people when Harmony carried out "gradual life support cutback"? GLSC. Schmidt imagined a conversation between Harmony officials. Said one: "Let's glitch the bastards." Said the other: "Yeah, let's glitch 'em, let's glitch 'em good."

On the left people in spic-and-span clothing streamed out of the lighted rectangle of a large concrete building, a Meditation Hall. They were gone in a flash as the van drove by, but they set Schmidt to thinking about the people on the Outside. Not the officials, the little people. How did they feel about the Confinements? America had become a remarkably quiet and placid place since the so-called "Renewal," that period of a year or more after Gunnison's take-over. They were said to resemble the Japanese of antediluvian times. (The Japanese resettlements on the Asian mainland were areas of turmoil, passion, and disorder. Class war raged. The Japanese had settled once and for all the argument about an unchangeable national character. There was no such thing.)

Americans operated the great industrial plant—for it remained great even after the disorders of 1999-2000. They farmed, raised cattle, moved goods, educated, communicated, and entertained themselves. But Harmony was not a world power, as the U.S. had been. Its financial and military tentacles were withdrawn and folded in a prim, clean lap. The striving, hustling, bustling spirit had gone out of Americans. All that they promoted now was the Confinements. Was that a clue? Had America withdrawn into itself to nurture a new-creation? Or was it caught in the grip of a fatal disease? Was American placidity a kind of grand, national guilt?

The car slowed down. Abruptly they were out of the holographic ghost town. The geometric uniformity of the real Manhattan lay behind. The scene resolved into an ancient neighborhood of half-ruined brick buildings, dark in silhouette against the barrier's shimmer. The road ahead had narrowed, and in the headlights of the vehicle Schmidt saw the huge buckled concrete slabs of an impassable street.

"We go on foot from here." The car door opened and a light came on in the cab of the van. Gilligan held the door. "You're absolutely safe," he said. Schmidt groaned a little as he got out.

Ancient bones. "We've got this whole place staked out with men." Gilligan gestured in a wide circle with an electric torch Schmidt hadn't seen him activate.

Schmidt stretched. He was still tired, despite the good snooze on the plane and a nap in the aseptic hotel room. The barrier was very near. It much resembled a rainbow, but it was a dome of a rainbow, not merely a strip. Tiny fireflies of current pulsed amidst the colors. It was beautiful in a way.

He followed the circle of Gilligan's light on the broken pavement, and they walked into the darkness of brick.

How the barrier was generated, the cost of generation, how deep it extended underground, and how high into the sky—all that had been in the brochures. They knew all about the deletenious gynomax expansion but nothing about the Lady of the Expansion.

The abandoned old-fashioned buildings turned out to be part of a buffer zone between the barrier and the rest of the city. In a moment they were through it and emerged into a no man's land. Gilligan hesitated—then moved to his left in a diagonal line across the razed terrain. In the jerkily moving ball of light, Schmidt saw bits of broken brick pressed into the clay, pieces of reinforcing bars dark with rust, and other litter. He had a wry thought. All this was a bit below par for the famous tidiness of New Harmony. Immediately up ahead the barrier seemed to rise right out of the ground.

Suddenly Schmidt stopped. "Hold it a minute, Mr. Gilligan!"

Gilligan turned and his light turned with him on the ground.

Schmidt gestured. "Who're they?"

The light moved and picked out a girl on the edge of the desolate, barren terrain. She stood near a brownstone that had been cut in half by the giant bulldozer that must have cleared this strip of land. Behind her a bathtub hung like a whitish blob inside the shell of the building by a pipe. The girl stood very erect, very still. Her blond hair fell straight down. She wore a simple skirt and blouse. Neatly neo-puritan. Beyond her stood another girl in the same attitude, and beyond her yet another, and so on until the desolation curved away out of sight.

Schmidt looked at Gilligan who hadn't replied. The young man fidgeted in obvious discomfort.

"Well?"

Gilligan hesitated, unsure of himself. Like every other official of the New Puritan Secular Order, he was an avid student of the Harmonizer's writings, but he didn't fully understand the doctrine of differential moral pressure that people used to explain the Vigil. To Gilligan the Vigil had always seemed a straightforward protest movement that should be put down without much ado, and that's how his superiors would behave, he thought, if they were free to act. But somehow a protest movement was not compatible with the doctrine of differential moral pressure. Anyway, Gilligan was confused.

"Girls," he said lamely, unable to delay any longer. "Just some girls."

Schmidt raised his eyebrows at the evasive reply. Girls they were, so much was established; but he didn't need Gilligan to tell him that. This was one hell of a lot more than girls. This was a formation of girls. The girls stood spaced out at five meter intervals. All stood in the same odd, almost reverent pose, Schmidt said:

"Surely that can't be all? Come on, Hank. You have such nice initials for everything that I don't understand. Tell me what the letters are."

Gilligan smiled, painfully. "That's the VOP," he said. He added: "If you must know." When Schmidt raised his eyebrows again, he went a step further: "The Vigil of Protest."

"Oh? I thought you people lived in harmony. All the malcontents are supposed to be behind that thing." Schmidt gestured at fireflies in a sea of color.

Inwardly Schmidt was pleased. Maybe the America he knew and loved hadn't died altogether. There was some hope.

Gilligan squirmed. "It's the Constitution," he said. He paused, struggling to find the right expression. "Oh, gee, it's complicated. You see, Karl, they're not organized. They never speak. They come alone; they leave alone. We've got agents tracking the lot, but we've never been able to prove conspiracy. So it's not a protest under the Constitution." Pause. "God knows *why* they do it . . . Of course we have a theory."

"Differential moral pressure? Unidentified co-vibrators?"

"Oh, you've been told."

"Enough to understand, altogether enough," Schmidt said. "Of course no one bothered to tell me about the . . . VOP. Why do they call it the Vigil of Protest?"

"*They* don't call it anything. *They* just come and stand here. The people call it that. It's just a phrase that's got about. We'd better be going, Karl."

"Just a minute," Schmidt said. "How long has this been going on?"

"As long as I can remember. I guess ever since the barrier went up. That'd be seven years."

"So not *all* the people support the Confinement—on the Outside, that is."

"I wouldn't say that," Gilligan protested. "Not a bit. Like you said, they're co-vibrators. They are attracted to the baseness." Gilligan gestured toward the barrier. "They rightfully belong in there. Could we go? This is the time they always start coming through. I don't want to miss the action."

Schmidt hesitated, but then he gave up, nodded, and followed Gilligan's light once more toward an unmarked hole in the middle of the razed terrain. Once it must have been the entrance to the subways that no longer ran.

They went down and then, led by Gilligan's light, they walked along abandoned corridors amidst cobwebs and litter to a small room crowded with equipment. Two lounging detectives rose and were introduced. Then Gilligan pointed to a large screen set against the wall. It showed the sparkling light of the barrier edged on two sides by what looked like a broken wall. They sat down to wait for a chief.

THE chief was a long time in coming. At the moment he—that is to say Emmanuel Toronto Salazar Smith—sat on a rock in a cavelike enclosure with his hands around his face. He sat on a white handkerchief that he had spread out to protect his suit. From time to time he glanced up at the shimmering barrier that filled the cave with dim light. He glanced especially at the fireflies in the color, measuring their intensity.

On two successive earlier tries, he had found the Fire too hot. Three chiefs had gone ahead of him, and it being the peculiarity of the Fire to intensify when someone passed through it, Manny-Man had had to wait. Now he still waited, guessing that in another hour or so he might chance it again.

He smoked his last cigarette like a man condemned. He carefully smoothed the empty package and put it in his pocket. Then he waited without even that consolation.

On the other side of the barrier, in the small observation room, the two detectives, accustomed now to the presence of the foreign visitor and bored by the absence of action on the flickering screen, resumed the argument Schmidt's entrance had interrupted. They discussed the Flood.

One maintained that the Flood had come because Ralph Waldo had prayed for Divine vengeance seeing that the Nation disregarded his counsel. Furthermore, the things that had gone on in California! The Devil himself had lived in California and had feasted his nostrils on the smoke of hippies and cats and children sacrificed by cultists on the beaches over fires of driftwood. It was no surprise to the detective that God should listen to Ralph's entreaties. He himself had known something would happen just from reading his Bible.

The second one called the first a superstitious fool whose blabberings were a blasphemy and degraded the Great Mental Scientist. He wouldn't sit by and let any man make a pretty tribal god out of Ralph Waldo. Ralph was the ultimate modern man—a man who'd learned the laws both of Matter and Spirit.

If this detective's opinion counted for anything, it was that Ralph had foreseen the Flood by searching the Future with his Third Eye, the one the Hindoos said was right in the center of your forehead and opened when you lived a strictly scientific life. As for the Bible, in his humble opinion, it was a corruption of something once valuable, but for all practical purposes, it was as good as useless now.

As this argument grew heated, Gilligan became slightly embarrassed and tried to engage Schmidt in a competing conversation. But Schmidt waved him away. He said this was a most interesting and enlightening discussion. Hearing this, the detectives launched into ever greater flights of eloquence.

Thus time passed.

At last, in his cave, Manny-Man rose from his rock. He thought he detected a thinning of sparkles in the color, and when he tested the Fire with a finger, he found that it had lessened its bite.

The third try would succeed, he decided. Three was the Lady's sacred number. This time he'd make it all the way through and not recoil from the suffocating nausea and searing, paralyzing pain.

He took a deep breath.

His fear had become so intense that his bod no longer felt it. Sweat beads stood on his forehead and over his lip. He moved forward, but his feet were rooted in the clay dirt of the ground. He stared down and saw bits of old tile that had paved this area.

"Please," he whispered. "Please, Lady, be with me, let me go, let it be over, please release me."

The lady denied his request. Instead she made him think compulsively about the passage back which was also still before him. He'd have to make it carrying a girl in his arms. And he remembered Betty Simple as they'd passed through coming the other way—not at this breach but at another. She had screamed in the middle of the hell of Fire. And he'd stared at her face, her open mouth, her terrified eyes. And Fire had clung to her lips and tongue and teeth. Her brows and hair and eyes had flamed. And he'd almost fainted with the fear of strangeness that had overcome his bod fear.

"Be with me, Lady," he whispered again.

He gave himself a little nudge forward, and this time his body obeyed him. He eased himself into the brilliant hell slowly, shoulder first, his face torn by a grimace. Centimeter by centimeter he merged with the barrier and became a dark shape within its brilliance.

Schmidt saw the figure first and called attention to it. It was a dark humanoid shadow in the light. It came very slowly. Then at last Manny-Man boke out of the barrier, doubled over, swayed, and fell over like someone dead. He jerked involuntarily. Spasms passed over his half-bent form. Whisps of electromagnetic energy played over the exposed surface of his skin like flames. Then the radiation died down to a shimmer on hands and face. Finally even the shimmer faded away.

"Peacefreak," Gilligan said, and the disputatious detectives nodded. "That's our man." Gilligan was tense with excitement. "The yellow tie," he added with a glance at Schmidt.

Schmidt marveled. The form on the ground testified to the excruciating agonies the slow passage must cause. Why did they do it? Surely only the deepest and most fundamental human motivation could induce a man to go through such torture.

Gilligan walked to a radio and called for someone he dubbed Dragnet Five. He told the man they had a "live one." He gave instructions and emphasized that no action be taken until the subject had committed an act of force. "We've got to have an honest to goodness V-P pair," he concluded. "You know those chicks. They know the Constitution. We've got to get them dead to rights." Dragnet Five said that he understood.

Gilligan then turned to Schmidt. "It's all set. This should be clean as a whistle." He pointed to the screen where the Peacefreak still spasmed on the ground. "He'll come to in about twenty minutes. Then he'll clean himself. They believe they must be spic-and-span to go undetected. They always pick a nice clean spot on this side. I'll give you odds that he'll go under the strip and come up in the brick. Then he'll snatch himself a VOP chick, I'd guess. He'll drag her back into the ruins. When he gets her into the shadows, we'll move in."

Gilligan was all serious concentration, all cop. He rubbed his hands.

"And then?" Schmidt asked.

"And then we'll vipple the pair."

III

THE girl waited to be snatched. Her name was Timmy McCallum, but in the Vigil they called her Rubeegol, which was the brandname of a lipstick. She also thought of herself as Rubeegol. She had left her old life behind.

Everyone in the Visible Vigil had a code name, the necessary condition for surreptitious communications by telephone and letter. Communications were essential, for the Vigil orchestrated a widespread national protest—and what it had become, the Expansion Plot. So the girls had code names, and the girlish chit-chat about nail-polishes, deodorants, depilatories, creams, ointments, unguents, and powders wasn't what it seemed.

But it was more complicated than that.

No member of the VV ever spoke to any other member, but they communicated nevertheless, using intermediaries, never fewer than three. The go-betweens were members of the Invisible Vigil.

These girls never went near the forty-seven Confinements of New Harmony.

Rubeegol came from the upper class. Her father belonged to the new aristocracy that had arisen with NPSO. He was Internal Crusade Representative for Allied Donsanto International, one of two chemical giants in the country with headquarters in flood-safe St. Louis in Mokan Harmony. Rubeegol grew up in California. She took part in the East Rush when, following the earliest California tremors in February 1999, a third of the state's population (later called The Remnant) had literally climbed the Rocky Mountains and had thus escaped both the earthquakes and the Flood. Her father had been a space engineer in charge of a thousand people engaged in the formulation of nose-cone coatings, and thus he had the management experience required for organizing one of the sixteen Remnant "Salients" that had fanned out all over the land east of the Rockies to generate the popular uprising in favor of Gunnison.

Through the first years of the Renewal, Rubeegol had been an ardent Puritan, working as a nurse in the Civil Disturbance. When things settled down, she resumed her interrupted studies, and since there was no longer a UCLA, she went to Eastcoast. Here she witnessed establishment of the first Confinement, and she was one of the first girls in her class to join the Women's Protest which over time grew into the Vigil.

Rubeegol served IV for nearly four years. She recruited eighty girls at last, and as a reward she was allowed to "take off her makeup," as they said in the Movement. She turned visible. She got her chance to enter Lady-service inside the barrier.

This was her three hundredth day of vigil. With days off and vacations counted in, that made nearly a year and a half of waiting—time enough to grow impatient, time enough to wonder if she'd ever be snatched.

Yet tonight she had a light heart. Beneath the hard-nosed militancy that came with the acceptance of Vigil discipline, Rubeegol remained a woman. She didn't totally avoid the pervasive anti-fem propaganda which said—in effect—that women were different: more sentimental, a little light headed, warmer of heart, ungifted in technology, and intuitive rather than brainy. She knew all this for the pure bosh it was. Rubeegol knew all about women and what they could do.

In a period of less than seven years, a handful of women (many of them active Puritans during the Renewal) had infiltrated the Confinements and established the Lady-cult. It had started as a collective effort, as a political tactic, a way to give cohesion and hope to the wretches in those unspeakable, bounded slums. But the Cult had developed a spirit and meaning of its own. The rituals devised to manage the masses had begun to act on the originators, and now the Cult was something more. The bits and pieces of poetry and scripture taken almost at random from hundreds of sources and Xeroxed crudely to make a Holy Book had linked like fibers into a real Scripture with an oddly cohesive logic of its own. The concept of a stern yet benevolent Lady—simultaneously Bride, Mother, and Ancient Crone—now seemed real and vibrant with life. Taboos imposed merely to create an air of mystery turned out now to have inherent value. (One of these was the sanctity of metals of all kinds, and the command to save them.) Disciplines extracted to create order had created high morale. (One of these was the requirement that chiefs undergo the Ordeal of Fire to get a queen and hence to merit their positions of leadership.) Oracular pronouncements by pack and tribal queens became of necessity real oracles. And the sacramental fornications on Janenights—chosen as a central rite because nothing less would have captured the attention of the debased population—had become charged with symbolic significance. The Lady became the Cosmos, the Ecosphere, the Mild Adaptation, the Circle of Peace, the Song of Heaven, the Merciful, the Bond of Service. Her robe was the sky and her undergarments the rainbow, and the barrier itself the shelter of her skirts.

In the Lady's name—and later in Her service—women worked to free the confined populations using any and all tools they could, including technical tools. Rubeegol stood on the edge of the razed terrain in shoes between whose soles cadmium flakes had been hidden. They would make solar panels, and the panels would power the underground factories. Her clothing was laced with other metals and fibers needed to make neutralizers. Progress was slow, but the first factory, the one beneath Sophia Grande in Eastcoast, already produced such devices. They couldn't be used yet. The authorities could detect neutralizer breaches. But they were being produced, and some day they would be used.

Rubeegol was all too conscious of the fact that women had organized the metals smuggling, bypassing the detectors at the official gates through the device—and the discipline—of Queen Raids. Women had engineered the logistical system Outside as well as the production system within. Women had solved the complex problems presented by an environment so primitive the common people burned fecal waste to cook their meals.

Women. Yes, women had done all that, a signal achievement. The Confinement had helped, of course. The psychic pressures generated by a population expanding against a barrier had prepared the folk for religious conversion. The brutal competition for food had created a longing for unity and peace—and the Lady-cult supplied a kind of central union even as it pardoned and sactioned the reality of vicious foodwar that it couldn't stop. Better that some live well than that all starve and Confinement become a graveyard of men and women without flesh on their bones. Meanwhile in every oracle every queen urged the people to make the Realm green.

Women. She was proud to be a woman.

Nevertheless, Rubeegol accepted from the Harmony propaganda what it pleased her to accept. She was superstitious when it pleased her, and she was more intuitive than men, when it pleased her. After all, she *was* a woman, and it was the ancient privilege of women to do what they pleased. She knew this in her bones.

Tonight it pleased her to have an intuition. She would be snatched. She knew it. It also pleased her to be superstitious. She felt she had received too omens. This was the three hundredth day of her vigil, and the number three was sacred to the Lady. The second omen had been a flashlight beam pointed in her direction by two men who'd stood in the darkness and had then disappeared down the subway entrance. The light had picked her out. Why her? Why not one of the other vigilantes? Rubeegol felt sure it was a sign.

She thought about that, and she thought about life inside the Realm, the year she'd spend inside a cage hung up in a church or chapel, the Janenights she'd announce whenever it pleased her, and then the work in Sophia Grande on the great plot to break out of the bubbles and overrun the land.

Her mind wandered off into the future and ranged over the past. She exulted in the thought that humanity would once again be reunited in America. The narrow, crabby aberration of a time would be swept away. But then she brought her mind back to her intuition, growing fidgety and nervous again. Her time was nearly up. She'd have to leave soon and then, after a measured interval, as if it had happened at random, another girl would take her place.

But no, she thought, that won't be. Tonight is the night.

It was in the air about her. She felt a sense of expectation.

Or was it just that the squeeze were thicker than usual? In that ruin to her left she'd seen the glow of a cigarette. Earlier she'd heard the upsurge and abrupt cut-off of a transistor radio—as if someone's finger had slipped on the volume dial. They were out in force tonight.

Well, she thought, they can't do anything to me.

Is it *that* that I'm sensing? she wondered, momentarily worried. All those cops?

No, she assured herself. It's real. I'll be snatched tonight.

The police were remarkably well disciplined, by and large. Nevertheless Rubeegol had heard of girls who'd been dragged off into the ruins by squeeze for a bit of forcible bushwack. She imagined a dirty old mattress, a heavy pressing body, hard breathing.

She shook off the feeling. It had never happened to her, but it was the kind of thing a vigilante was supposed to take in her stride. You couldn't be sexually selective in the job. You'd be the mate of whatever chief snatched you, even if he turned out to be Frankenstein himself.

Time passed.

Rubeegol watched the play of fire in the barrier. An airplane flew by overhead. She grew sluggish and despondent. And when the feet dislodged a brick behind her in the ruin, she mistook the sound for the scamper of a rat. The man caught her totally by surprise. His final rush came too quickly to elicit anything resembling a reaction from her. The hand enveloped her mouth and crushed her nose. She gulped for air. A knee bruised the small of her back. Her hands fought frantically for balance as he pulled her back. Then she saw an explosion of stars. The pain rushed in just as her consciousness fled.

SHE came awake in a speeding car. She opened her eyes for a second and immediately closed them again. One glimpse told her that she was in a police van. She lay on a cot. Peripherally she'd sensed another figure next to her, and at the foot of the cot had squatted a police technician in a white shirt. She'd recognized the gold-rimmed cap. In the wide front seat she'd seen two men next to a driver in a chauffeur's uniform.

The tactic of camouflage rewarded her with information. The men in the front conversed, and she could hear them fairly well despite the rush of tires on the pavement.

"Mind you," one voice said—it was bright, young and eager. "We don't know for sure that it'll work, but our psychologists swear it'll incapacitate the man."

"By the expansion of his consciousness. I was told that; over dinner." The voice of an older man. Rubeegol detected an accent.

Silence. The wheels whizzed over pavement.

Rubeegol felt a dull ache on the side of her head, a throbbing. But she pushed that aside. She was thinking hard. She added one and one together. She had been snatched. In the moment before some hard object had exploded against her head, she'd known her attacker as a chief. By the smell. Not a cop, a chief. The pungent odor still hung in the car. It conjured up a flash-memory of her uncle's farm. Men coming in from the hunt brought in that earthy odor, that redolence of animality. The figure she sensed next to herself must be a chief and her attacker.

Adjustment operation, she thought with irritation. Clumsy attempt to influence the internal politics of the Confinement. It irritated Rubeegol because it meant a delay in her entry, nothing more. They would lecture the chief and, if it pleased them, they'd include her also under the 'victim' rubric of the law. At most they could carry on for twenty-three hours and fifty-nine minutes. Thereafter it was detention, and that was unconstitutional. Then they'd be released or placed inside EC. She preferred release. If she was pushed through the metal detectors at the official entry point, she would lose the previous cargo she carried.

Up front the older man spoke: "You've assured me that it's legal, but I've been thinking. In Berlin we'd call it an invasion of privacy. Isn't that illegal here?" A foreigner, hence the accent.

"Not if it's mutual," the young voice said. "The Celestial Arbiters found that an *exchange* of privacies was not covered."

Rubeegol was puzzled. What on earth were they talking about now. An exchange of privacies? It sounded menacing, somehow.

"Doesn't that come to the same thing?" Berlin asked. "It hurts them both, doesn't it? And even if we assume that the perpetrator deserves what he gets—what about the victim? Those failure rates you cited earlier don't sound encouraging. Not for mice or rats or hamsters or guinea pigs; certainly not for people. You're exposing an innocent victim to the high risk of schizophrenia. High risk, if your numbers are correct."

"Innocent?"

"Of course. The victim's innocent, of course."

"We have a slightly different conception here," the young voice said. "We make no differentiation."

Now Rubeegol understood a part of what they

were talking about. Ralphy's Science of Morals, she thought. The victim invites the crime. Nothing ever happens by accident. If you get robbed, you *want* to get robbed. The Mind reaches out and grabs hold of Substance. Substance manifests in Phenomena. She thought of the ideological indoctrination she'd undergone during the Renewal and later in college. It had all made marvelous sense at one time.

The older man said: "I had forgotten. That is your penological doctrine. That falls under the rubric of co-vibration, right? But I'd understood that you don't carry that principle into practice. Say a high official of NPSO is attacked, what then?"

Rubeegol began to like the old man.

The youngster answered: "As a rule we don't enforce that provision, and there is the exception clause where a victim can show that professional or scientific involvement with crime may have been the cause of the attack. But the point is, Karl, that we're legally covered. That's why we don't hesitate to vipple the girl. Legally she's as guilty as the man."

"Mr. Gilligan, I—"

But Rubeegol didn't hear what the older man said. The car ran over a ribbed surface now and tires hummed at a high pitch. She recognized the place by the sound. Good old familiar Police Compound. It was like home. They dragged you off to the Compound once a month at least for interrogation. They were on the West Side near Seventh Avenue and Thirty-Third Street.

The phrase rang though her mind. *Vipple the*

girl. Vipple? Rubeegol began to feel strong apprehensions and judged it high time to come awake officially. She opened her eyes and looked about, sat up. There was a chief beside her, a handsome, dark brute of a man—not Frankenstein, thank God. Her movement appeared to trigger motion in the technician who squatted at the foot of her cot. He reached down into a narrow black case between his legs.

"Where am I? What is this? Where are you taking me?"

She spoke calmly knowing the rules of the game. At her words the two men in the front seat immediately turned and the chauffeur glanced over his shoulder briefly. She saw an expression of sympathy in the grey eyes of the older man, but the young one looked stern. He said:

"Calm yourself, chicky. Just don't get hysterical right away."

"I'm not a bit hysterical. I just want to know where you're taking me."

The young man turned to the technician who still fumbled with something between his knees. "Messerschmidt, you better give her a sedative. She's overwrought."

"Now just a minute," Rubeegol cried, but she saw that it would do no good to argue. The technician had risen to a crouching position and approached her with an injector in his hand. His round cap almost brushed the roof of the van and he swayed with the motion of the vehicle. She struggled briefly when he bent over her, but the gun soon touched her arm at one point, and for the second time within a short span she felt the outrush of awareness.

THE VPLE laboratory's action component was a room divided in the center by a pane of glass. One side contained two elaborate devices that reminded Schmidt of dentist's chairs. An impressive console stood between them. Wires ran from the console to instrument arms above each chair. On the other side of the glass were armchairs, couches, a coffee table, and other furniture reminiscent of a doctor's waiting room.

Dr. Fieldgreen, a little man in a white coat and sporting a goatee, stood by the glass with Schmidt on the couch side. Gilligan leaned over the coffee table behind them and leafed through a magazine. Beyond the glass, lab technicians prepared the V-P pair. Both the girl and the dark man were unconscious, and the technicians strapped them into the chair now.

Dr. Fieldgreen apologized for the seeming simplicity of the set-up. He had a calm, precise delivery. "There is much, much more to VPLE than you see here," he assured Schmidt. "Our computer facilities are on the floor below, and the signal modulators occupy sixty cubic meters on the floor above." He pointed a finger at the white cork of the sound-proofed ceiling. "The rest of this floor is office space, labs, and the animal test areas, of course. Our annual budget is eighty-five million dollars, but of course we spend most of that in outside contracts on component work. You see, Herr Schmidt, we are still looking for improvements This process takes almost eight hours, which is unacceptable, totally unacceptable." Dr. Fieldgreen frowned and shook his head to underline his words.

"How do you monitor the process," Schmidt

asked. He had been toying with an idea he didn't care to share with anyone just yet.

"Through instruments," the doctor said. "I failed to mention that, but we have a recording room next door where the wave patterns are graphed."

"I meant," Schmidt pursued a little guardedly, "I meant human monitoring. Can't you . . . I guess I'd imagined that you could 'listen in' on the exchange between two people. Human monitoring . . ."

The little man shook his head slowly but persistently. "No, no," he said. "No, no, Herr Schmidt." He lifted a finger. "First, it's highly dangerous. The danger of schizoid reaction is pronounced. In that area, we are also expending some resources, as you can imagine. Second," and he added another finger, "there's what we call the Heisenberg effect. You see, Herr Schmidt, you can't monitor without participation, and so the monitoring itself would tend to interfere with the process. Third—"

"Excuse me, Doctor. I didn't understand you completely. You mean to say you don't know *what* is exchanged between the people?"

"Of course we do. Their life experience." Dr. Fieldgreen pointed to the couple in the dentist chairs. Technicians were fitting loose nets of wire over the man' head. "*His* experience will become *her* experience, and *her* memories, feelings, etc., will become *his* memories and so forth."

"Do you mean that he'll lose his memories and get hers?" Schmidt asked increduously.

"No, no. Each will retain his or her memories as well. The process is additive."

"Hmm," Schmidt said, thinking. "But as for substance, the content of those memories. Do you monitor . . ."

"We have no way of monitoring that—unless, of course, we were to subject ourselves to VPLE, which is ridiculous."

"Then how do you know what takes place?"

"Through animal tests."

"But how can you be sure? One animal picks up what another animal has learned?"

"Exactly. After VPLE each has the other's behavioral repertoire."

Schmidt shook his head in wonder. If it was true, if it really worked, this device could fantastically magnify human powers.

"Third," Dr. Fieldgreen said.

Schmidt looked at him in puzzlement. Then he saw the three fingers in the air.

"One more question, Dr. Fieldgreen, before you go on to your third point. Dr. Fieldgreen, has it occurred to you that VPLE might create a superman?"

The doctor nodded. "It has. But we don't think it will. It hasn't created a supermouse or a superrat at this point. As a matter of fact, the tendency is in the other direction. Vippled laboratory animals tend as a whole to underperform in the maze. We have a theory about that. We call it the Field Capacity Syndrome. We assume, and I think rightly, that the brain can only absorb and hold so much information—what we call field capacity. And if it's overloaded, you get a leaching effect. The additional input seeps away. That seems to be the actual situation. Two sets of experience get mixed up, but only a portion of each remains, and consequently the subject loses mental coordination. At least that was the obvious result with Abe Herzenberg Sultzy Chico Kid."

Abe Herzenberg Sultzy Chico Kid. Superrats and supermice. Mental leachate dripping through the psychic ether. A strange world, Karl Schmidt thought, which made mice and rats the model for Man assuming no discontinuity in the spectrum of life between rodent and poet. Maybe there was no sharp and obvious break. Maybe man was nothing more than a superrat . . .

"Third," Dr. Fieldgreen said.

Schmidt gave the persistent doctor a glance. "Oh. Of course. Third, Dr. Fieldgreen."

"Third," said the doctor, "we couldn't monitor even if we could. That would be an illegal invasion of privacy."

"Why, of course," Schmidt said. "I'd forgotten about that."

DR. FIELDGREEN threw the switch shortly after midnight. The instrument panel on the console between the chairs came alive in multichromatic splendor. In the chairs the man and girl seemed unaware that anything had transpired. They sat strapped in, asleep or comatose, their faces even and peaceful as if they were dreaming. Each had a netting draped about the head with wires extending from the netting to the instrument arm and from there to the console. Furthermore, Schmidt understood that the impulse from *her* chair passed, through the console, into the signal modulator banks on the floor above; and from there, presumably modulated, to the computer banks on the floor below; and from there, appropriately digitalized, into the console; and from there, through the cables, to his chair. And vice versa.

Schmidt watched, wondering if he would have a chance to do the foolish thing he had decided to do.

The large group that had assembled soon dispersed again. There was nothing to see, no drama, no action. Nevertheless, Schmidt continued standing before the glass, his arms folded in front, his eyes on the couple. He was aware that his continued presence was a bother to both Gilligan and Dr. Fieldgreen.

At a quarter to one, Gilligan appeared at his elbow and suggested that they retire now. The process would continue until eight in the morning, there would be no change . . .

But Schmidt shook his head.

First, his personal body-clock now said that it was nearly seven in the morning in Berlin, the time he habitually rose without the help of an alarm. Soon he would get up and put on his thick blue-white robe. In the refrigerator would be a cool carton of yogurt. Five after seven the bell would ring and Rudi, the baker's son, would bring him hot, crisp rolls.

Second, Schmidt was much too interested in this process to abandon the scene now.

He told Gilligan this much, leaving out the yogurt part. Then he tapped the young man on the shoulder in a fatherly way. "Go on home and get a good rest," he said. "You probably have a wife waiting for you."

Gilligan blushed a little. It appeared that he had

no wife. He was only thirty-two, and ani-fer asked you not to marry until thirty-five.

"However that may be," Schmidt said, "please feel free to go."

And third, he thought. But the real reason why Schmidt wanted to stay he kept to himself.

Gilligan accepted the verdict and somewhat morosely he sat down on the couch and picked up the magazine he had been reading. It was the latest issue of *The Meditative Scientist*. The lead article was "Gunnison's Contributions in Mental Chemistry."

A little after two in the morning, Gilligan finally gave up his vigil. He rose and told Schmidt that, if it was all right with him, he'd slip off and grab a nap in the BDQ where he lived. Schmidt told him he'd made a wise decision and asked what BDQ stood for. Bachelor Detective Quarters, Gilligan told him. The BDQ was just a hop and a skip from here, and Gilligan had the phone number of his room written out on a slip of paper torn form a page of the magazine. Call him anytime. Then he bade good night and left.

Still Schmidt waited.

Apart from the hum of machinery and the on-and-off throb of an air compressor somewhere overhead, there was very little activity in the VPLE laboratory. At half past two Dr. Fieldgreen put in an appearance and stayed for a short chat. He parted saying that he'd be unavailable for a while. His assistant, Miss Virginia Haut, could be reached by pushing that button just to the left of the Harmonizer's picture on the wall. Miss Haut spoke German like a native, Dr. Fieldgreen said, as if to encourage Schmidt, and then he also left.

Miss Haut did not make an appearance, but Schmidt noted that a technician entered the action room in half hour intervals, glanced at instruments, and made marks on a sheet affixed to a clipboard.

After a while Schmidt went to the toilet and, on the way, he looked around a bit. He opened a door here and glanced into a room there, and he saw that the place was empty. For a while he contemplated pairs of rats wired in gleaming glass containers as they exchanged lives. A paper-cluttered office with wood paneling would be Dr. Fieldgreen's domain. Over the doctor's desk he saw a clock. The time was nearly four.

Schmidt went back to the waiting room just in time to see the technician enter with his clipboard. Schmidt watched while inside his fifty-nine year chest his heart beat like that of a nine-year-old. At last the technician took his leave, and Schmidt took a deep breath to calm himself. He squared his shoulders and walked through the glass door in the glass wall disregarding the DO NOT ENTER SIGN.

IV

EMMANUEL Toronto McCallum Salazar Rubeegol Timmy Smith whirled away into celestial agonies and then dropped down again like a leaf abandoned by the breeze. And then the breeze came back again and carried the androgynous Creature up again in a spiral through corridors of fusing experience . . . back, back, back once more to that which had been, until the plasticities of perception collapsed again and the Creature fell in a darkness down, down, down . . . but never far enough down, never down to the dark, still, limpid rest for which it longed.

It was a roller-coaster to exhaustion. Each successive pass penetrated deeper and fused ever more experience. Cell clusters fell into the relentless wine press of some kind of electronic force and gave up the juices of memory, and a male juice mingled with a female juice and dried on parched vistas of bruning nerve deserts into visions.

The Creature seethed with an enormity of insight. It longed to stop and to assess the fantastic experience. Its fused parts started dialogues constantly interrupted by brutal shoves into yet other, deeper, and stranger tangles of recall. On the ends of the whirling, egg-shaped mental cosmos cracks began to form. The Creature sensed in panic that those cracks might open and drain away the last cohesion of its being. Its structure of awareness groaned in the final stages of a pleasure so intense that it was a searing pain.

Stop, screamed the Creature, falling once more, falling into a black darkness of total exhaustion. Stop, it screamed. I can't stand it any more.

And it stopped, Incredibly, it stopped.

The Creature fell. It was a leaf in the shaft of a deep well. The orange-red blaze of experience was a receding circle of light above. It came down slowly, turning. It came to rest on the still surface of a motionless sea.

For a timeless moment the Creature braced for the inevitable kick of forces that would spiral it up from its floating bed into a thousand tortures of mingling, but the kick didn't come. The Creature lay softly and there was only a wondrous silence all about.

In that stillness and in that darkness, the Creature shaped an ego from the chaos by an act of reflection, and it discovered itself to be Emmanuel Salazar, a Puerto Rican male, lately the leader of a clump of humanity inside a penal reservation on the island of Manhattan. For sound but unconscious reasons, Salazar also used numerous other names, including the patronymic 'Smith,' whose purpose, he realized, was to set him apart and to enhance his authority with the suggestion of Anglo ancestry. He ruled by a combination of skill and instinct—a magnetic personality, quick executive reflexes, and an instant conceptual grasp of small-unit warfare. He commanded respect and won high shares of the Man's food distribution, and therefore he was the key element in Brinco Pack's survival. Through some kind of mechanical contrivance, the Eastcoast police had exposed him to the inner experience of the girl he had chosen for his fifth Queen, and he knew this because she knew it. He assumed that Rubeegol also knew what he knew. She was the agent of a Movement they called Lady-cult inside the Confinement, and the network embraced, by Salazar's calculation, at least fifteen percent of all women Outside. Within a short time, perhaps less than a year, by his calculations—combining what he knew (and now, for the first time, really understood) and what she knew—all of the Confinements in New Harmony would burst open like seedpods and engulf a surprised and unsuspecting world. From the ensuing collision would come—by inference from historical, cultural, anthropological, and psychological studies that Rubeegol's mind had furnished him as evidence—a great cultural efflorescence.

Salazar smiled at the bottom of the well cradled in a leaf on the measureless ocean of darkness. He retraced the mingling with Rubeegol's mind and now, in that stillness, he understood the process itself and how the fusion of memories had taken place. Unaware of the mechanism, he had resisted the experience with all of his ego energies, and in the process he'd almost destroyed the structure of his mind. If he ever had to do it again, he would know what to do. He'd cast aside all resistance and plunge with a cry of abandon into the alien mind—so very much the same as his own, so very much One and inseparably human.

And then he saw the dot of orange light at the top of the well grow in diameter until it became a blazing sun that came down toward him with a rush of light and fire, and he plunged eagerly into the kind, surprised, but welcoming mind of Karl Schmidt, Superintendent of the Berlin Police.

THE LONG arm of the clock on the wall moved dangerously close to the six. Schmidt expected the technician to come in any second with the clipboard.

Don't go yet. Salazar's mind said to him. *Give her time to recover and to consolidate her ego.*

There was a kind of laughter in the mind, a joyousness, an anticipation. He loves her, Schmidt thought.

Of course I love her, Salazar laughed. *How can you help but love someone you are.*

They both knew that Rubeegol's mind had swayed on the brink of collapse when Schmidt had at last released her for the leaf-like drop to the bottom of the well. They also knew that, given time, she'd make the same discoveries as Salazar had made, for she knew what he knew. Her impact on Schmidt had been far more brutal than Salazar's. Schmidt had clutched his head at the temples when the force pulled him into the panoramas of her being. He had reared back like an epileptic with the shock. The man, by contrast, was in control. He gave of himself or he denied as he wished. He could carry on a conversation or wander about Schmidt's memories taking this and leaving that. The power of his mind enveloped Schmidt and made the old man marvel at the potentialities of the human brain. But time was running out. The consequence of a discovery were more hazardous than the benefit of another minute's rest for Rubeegol. Schmidt thought "Good-bye" to Salazar and removed the netting from his head. He replaced it carefully over the girl's blond hair and then, furtively, like a fifty-nine year schoolboy, he slipped out through the door into the waiting room.

He'd left just in time. The technician entered and made for the gauges on the instrument console between the chairs. He lingered somewhat longer than usual, and his face darkened with puzzlement. He glanced at Rubeegol. He moved to her side. He removed and then replaced the netting on her head. Finally, back at the console, he nodded to himself and made a notation on his board.

Schmidt sought the comfort of the couch, sank down, and closed his eyes. He smiled to himself, rich with information about the Eastcoast Confinement. He, she, and Salazar knew something perhaps no one else knew so well—the shape of the future. He knew less than they did, of course. He'd only gotten a brief, confused glimpse, but it had been enough to cheer him. Schmidt also hoped that the glimpse of *him* that was now theirs would have a balmful influence—like a vitamin or other vital trace element—in the growth of the

Movement. He was sure that both of them would play major, perhaps decisive, roles in its future.

The experience had drained him, although it was still early. At the moment, in Berlin, it went on toward eleven in the morning—almost time to walk down to Cafe Mayer where, in company of men who had long retired, Schmidt took a cup of coffee, a small brandy, and granted himself a single cigar. Mid-morning. He dozed off.

Gilligan returned at seven-thirty restored to a pink, scrubbed, cheerful self full of eagerness to please. He brought a thermos of coffee for Herr Schmidt and a sweet roll. At a quarter to eight Dr. Fieldgreen walked through the waiting room muttering to himself. He clutched a set of paper discs marked by squiggly lines. He came back through again and then yet once more, until Gilligan stopped him and asked what it was that bothered him so.

"Back to the drawing boards," Dr. Fieldgreen muttered. He slapped a set of disks with a limp hand. "There is an inexplicable change in the pattern. It happened between four and four-thirty. We can't figure it out." He glanced at Schmidt. "Did you observe anything, Herr Schmidt?"

Schmidt shook his head slowly. "I'm afraid I won't be much help. After Mr. Gilligan left me in a lurch last night, I confess I followed his example and fell asleep on the couch." He smiled. "Sorry."

"Damnable pattern," Fieldgreen muttered, staring down at the disk. "It's almost as if . . ." He shook his head and walked out again.

At eight o'clock the entire VPLE laboratory staff arrived for the conclusion of the exercise. They crowded around the glass of the observation room while inside technicians uncoupled the victim-perpetrator pair. Schmidt stood at the window pretending consuming interest, but he already knew the strategy the couple would follow, something that he had worked out in a nano-second exchange of thought between himself and Salazar.

It all went as planned. The couple acted disoriented, sluggish, and stupid. Everyone beamed on Schmidt's side of the glass and exchanged pleased nods and glances. Just like Abe Herzenberg Sultzy Chico Kid. Unresisting, the couple let itself be led into the van. Then, with Schmidt and Gilligan up front again, the group drove in early morning light—it was overcast now—through the much diminished shimmer of holographic images north to the edge of the Confinement.

Detectives pushed the couple out of the van on the periphery of the brick. It looked far more dreary and desolate to Schmidt than it had in the rainbow-shimmer of the night. Before the van backed away again, leaving the pair outlined against the ruins, both he and she contrived to shoot a glance of full awareness to Schmidt, a look only the three of them understood.

The van backed away, turning. It lurched forward, backed again in the narrow road, and then it pulled away toward the concrete geometricities of Manhattan.

Emmanuel Salazar looked at the girl and she looked at him. Her face was his face, and he could read her eyes almost as if they were his own. There was still a little strangeness about her. He didn't know all about her; he hadn't plumbed her deepest being. The German had saved them. He had interrupted the process, and they both retained unviolated sanctuaries of irreducible privacy. His mind wheeled with the enormity of the task ahead, and he sensed that she had the same thought. So much to do. Harmony's new technology must be replicated. Raiding chiefs must be protected from the VPLE experience. Greater cohesion must be created within. Forces must be freed for production work. Time was of the essence. They had to win the race against GLSC. A track opened before his mental eyes. Soon he'd be chief of Peacefreak Tribe and later chief of chiefs. The process would be inevitable. He felt within him the fire and eloquence to move hearts, the will to overcome, and the intelligence to see the answers. And Rubeegol would remain his partner and mate throughout. She'd become the Lady's surrogate, She of the Visible Expansion. Together they would link the Confinements into a coordinated whole. She'd rule the temple, and he'd rule the war. He saw a flickering in her eyes, and with gladness he dropped these thoughts and smiled at her in response.

"You know, of course, that I love you."

"I never would have guessed," she said.

They embraced and kissed. When they broke apart, she said:

"No, darling, I won't scream in the Fire like Betty Simple did."

"That's encouraging," he said. "And I promise that I'll bathe occasionally."

"I'd call that progress," she said.

"Come on," he said, "after a night like this, I can hardly wait to get to know you."

"What've you got in mind," she asked. "A Janenight in the morning?"

"No, no. I don't particularly care to be watched. Let's have a dry run."

"Not too dry," she said, and they both laughed.

IT WAS the summer of 2008, a perfectly ordinary year. On July 19th of that year, at 2:49 in the afternoon, Berlin's Superintendent of Police boarded Lufthansa's Flight 301 for the transatlantic trip to Germany—and lest the old man get the wrong impression, a delegation of Eastcoat officials followed him all the way to the end of the ramp of Peaceful Abiding International Airport's international terminal.

Karl Schmidt stood before them, tall, grave, his long face kindly. He had been briefed, he had been toured, and now he assured the gentlemen that he had seen a very, very impressive display of American ingenuity. Yes, indeed, he said, America was and remained the land of promise, the beacon of the future. The officials were clearly pleased, and they waved to him as he boarded the jumbo jet. Hank Gilligan walked into the plane with him and made sure that he had a pillow and that his hat was properly put away into the overhead rack. Then, tears in his eyes, he shook hands with the German and, with a sob, turned and walked out.

The plane took off and flew away east. Soon it plunged into the night that came rushing west.

Schmidt did not sleep this time. He spent some hours on Level II, in the lounge, with a bottle of wine. He chatted with the senior stewardess. He enjoyed a light, Continental dinner. He browsed through some European newspapers he hadn't seen in days and caught up on all the latest scandals, abductions, and civil disturbances. Finally he walked up the stairs to the observation room of the tripledecker jumbo. He took up a position in front of one of the large oval windows, folded his arms across his back, and reflected on the mysterious unfolding of destiny.

Strange, he thought, very strange.

Inadvertently, unconsciously—or perhaps inspired by a kind of madness that is really the ultimate in sanity—Ralph Waldo Gunnison had stumbled onto the solution, one solution. He had intensified the disunities, separations, fragmentations, hatreds, and alienations that plagued the world. He had magnified the global disease to a point where man's genius at last found an answer. A new culture grew like a fetus inside the womb of Confinement, and it would burst forth soon, its face still shrouded, its character unrevealed. For a while there would be turmoil and the clash of forces old and new; but then the world would hear a new song and march to a new drumbeat.

Schmidt knew what he would tell the Senate. Wait, he'd say to them. Wait a couple of years. Oh, yes. Plan by all means. Plan in a low-key sort of way. Don't announce it to the public. Planning would take the Senate's attention off the issue. It would set their mind at ease about the future. And the future, Schmidt knew, would be revealed soon. In two years there would be no longer any Confinements on earth.

The huge machine hummed competently

through the darkness. In the sky stars hung in silence, unmoving. Then, suddenly, much sooner than he had expected, dawn drew a bright line across the horizon.

PLUTONIUM

I

IN HIS NINTH EXISTENCE he was an SS-guard at the infamous Hermsberg and acquired a heavy karmic debt.

In those days his name was Helmust Schweinhirt and in appearance he was chunky, blond, wide-faced, and steady.

On the cosmic scale, his Schweinhirt incarnation was already well above the average. Slowly he had grown in consciousness choosing ever more alert and discriminating parents. The Schweinhirt elders were peasants, but of the enterprising kind. *Mutti* ran a small vegetable shop supplied from *Vati's* suburban land where everything was raised by the most modern methods.

Helmut was well on his way up the ladder of awareness when the war came with its irresistible temptations. Then chaotic, psychic maelstrom caught him up and carried him along—from home to barracks to parade ground to Hermsberg, and he lived the evanescent dream of racial superiority for a second or two of eternal duration.

In the small room he rented near the concentration camp (Hermsberg was new and there were no barracks initially), he had two lamps shaded by tatooed human skin. Underneath the heavy, lumpy mattress of his narrow bed, in a small blue sack, he collected gold teeth and other curiosities.

Helmut was not unusually cruel or sadistic with the exception of one case, which would prove his undoing for some centuries to come. But he allowed himself to be carried away by the breathless lust of his comrades, a lust for violence which came and went in pulses over the camp, the consequence of frustration, ennui, guilt, and fear. Then he too joined in the beatings and tramplings of newly arrived Underhumans.

The temptation that would indirectly cost him his life some time later came one winter morning in the form of a father and his daughter. The father was a poet or lawyer or doctor, an inordinately tall figure, though a little stooped. He had curly salt-and-pepper hair; large, dark, watery eyes; and fingers of exceeding length. His eyes were mournful and heavy with awareness.

Helmut met the pair upon arrival, mingled in with others in a long stream of people reaching back to the cattle cars. In the reception hall men and women were split into separate groups, and Helmut stood there with several others amidst the odors of disinfectant, pushing the people along, making them move on, move on. A disturbance in another room called away the NCO in charge. During that unsupervised moment, Helmust approached the tall jew's daughter—she stood quite near him, eyes on the rough concrete floor—and he more or less fored her to yield up a kiss or two while his hands ranged indecently over her tits and under her skirt. She struggled fiercely.

She was something of a rarity in Hermsberg—a beauty. Bosomy, languid-eyed, long-lashed, and soft. Her skin and bearing spoke of silks and laces and recently lost wealth. Such as she seldom made it into this line. They were diverted to 'domestic service' in the homes of higher-ups. She would also be discovered, as Helmut knew quite well, and he wanted to get a feel of her while he had a chance.

Across the room the tall jew broke from the line so swiftly that the guards—who smirkingly enjoyed Helmut's antics with the pretty jewess—had no time to restrain him. He came in giant strides across the room, dark eyes burning, a little stooped. His exceedingly long, fine fingers grasped Helmut's blond locks, knocking Helmut's cap askew. He jerked back Helmut's head. Helmut yelled in pain and let go of the soft female. He turned to the tall jew with fury. The jew, still holding Helmut's hair, hit him across the face with a free hand—once, twice, three times. Guards grabbed the jew and dragged him away.

All day long his fellow guards teased Helmut about his humiliation. That night he sat alone in the light of a tatooed lamp and brooded with a book on his lap. The book dealt with infantry tactics, knowledge he would soon need. But he didn't read and didn't learn. He brooded about vengeance and about the soft jewess whose faint, sweet scent still seemed to cling to his cheek. She was . . . she seemed. . . . Oh, he didn't really know. She seemed so familiar to him. Kissing her had been the most natural thing in the world.

He soon succeeded in being assigned to a land-clearing party that included the tall jew. Decades later Hermsberg would be the site of a uranium mine, its product moving to Russia. Now it was a tiny village, a concentration camp, and a road in process of being built through the forest. The land-clearing work had to do with that road.

Outdoor duty was not exactly sought. Winter advanced on every front with snow and frost. Even bundled up in a heavy jacket and wearing a woolen cap beneath the helmet, a man froze out there, on the stone, icy ground. Mitted hands had to be slapped and boots had to be stamped to keep up the circulation in the extremities. The breath vapored whitely. The moisture froze in the nose. But Helmut felt no regret. He restored his German manhood methodically, repaying the slaps he had received with interest.

They spent some weeks together in cruel union. The man's name was Mahler, and he came from Berlin. Until this time those sensitive long fingers of his had never grasped anything more substantial than a pen. Now they were obliged to swing a pickaxe against soil so hard sparks seemed to fly from the contact of metal and earth. At any moment a blow might strike him from the side or from behind delivered with the stock of a rifle. Sometimes a kick sent him sprawling and his unprotected, gloveless, frozen hands bled when he rose, trembling from cold and malnutrition. Helmut's wide face and steady eyes would stare at him with satisfied menace.

"*Eines Tages, kleiner Helmut, eines Tages . . .*" Mahler would murmur with mournful eyes. The words mean, "One of these days, little Hel-

mut, one of these days . . ." He said them knowing that more blows would follow, said them
wanting blows. Mahler longed for an end to his
miseries. Blows, kicks, cold, hatred, indigestible
food, savage work in frozen wilderness—all these
would speed him to that eternal nothingness
which would follow the dissolution of this
wretched biological accident called Mahler.

The girl's name was Eva. Much as Helmut had
suspected, she had been segregated from the rest,
had disappeared into the quarters of a major. To
know her there, in someone else's arms, aroused
him to cold fury, and that fury left him in the form
of kicks and blows and cruelties, until Herr Mahler could no longer work and lay supine on his flat
straw, dead for all intents and purposes except for
a dark shining in his eyes.

By the mysterious channels of communications
that transcended all barriers between gentile and
jew, word of her father's treatment finally reached
Eva. Abruptly Helmut found himself with orders
to the Russian front.

It happened on the outskirts of Stalingrad.
Helmut was running for cover past the face of a
low-squatting peasant hut when a tiny, wizened,
wrinkled old fellow—he was clearly an old jew
with a tall black hat and sideburns curly at the
ends—appeared around the end of the building.
Helmut hesitated for a second, and that hesitation
was enough. He was caught by a plaster-blasting
string of machine-gun bullets and fell face down
on the ground. The final vision of his incarnation
was that of Eva's angry, frightened eyes when he
had violently sought the parted softness of her
lips.

He found himself in dimensionless paradise, a play of light and energies. Hurricanes of force caught and carried him. He struggled and fought, panicked, disoriented, and discovered that he had no arms to wave about, nothing tangible attaching to his free awareness. Terror grasped him. For a timeless moment he remembered all his lives, saw Eva in many incarnations, always his, always together, meant for each other, joined eternally. But this time he had lost her. The gradually ascending curve of his karma suddenly sagged in his German life, heavy with debt. He sucked nonexistent breath into nonexistent lungs.

I will do good, he thought, I'll pay it all back with a life of service.

At this thought a brightness formed above him, a brilliant light somewhere in that space that had no 'where' and no 'space.' A circle of light. It seemed to have a face, seemed to resemble the wrinkled old jew. It shone. The light frightened him, made him recoil. He turned, in a manner of speaking, toward the separated red of the spectrum around that disc of brilliance. He turned father, toward a purple, and then images began to form and lift from a gathering darkness.

He saw America, the New World. He knew it was America although at first it was nothing more than a vast continental darkness with a scatter of light along the coasts and here and there inland. From that sprinkled darkness a dark, chtonic force rose and pulled him down. On twenty million beds, carseats, haypiles, floors, couches . . . forty million Americans copulated on this Wednesday night—naked, half-naked, and almost fully clothed—in the manner of the two-backed beast, like dogs, side by side, and in unspeakable poses.

Desire!

He fell into the tornado of desire down below, drawn by mysterious forces, once more nearly encased in time but not yet securely material. His entire being longed for materiality, burned to participate in the creative act. But he wouldn't plunge in just anywhere. He sought among these copulators for cleanliness and innocence, for decency and righteousness, impelled away from the petty horror that had been his last life.

A dark-purple force-stream guided him in a westerly direction. The rising vibrations were benevolent as he descended. He plunged in precisely at the moment of impregnation, *was* the impregnation, his soul-force adding the tiny increment of energy the tailed semen needed to penetrate the giant ovum's resistant skin.

His mom and dad lay side by side, still breathing hard after the exertions of love, when the entity known as Helmut Schweinhirt—its cast-off body stiffening slowly against a Russian wall—dissolved in childish bliss and lost its memories.

The choice of the Clark identity turned out felicitous. To all appearances, the bad karma had been eradicated or would soon be displaced by the cumulations of service.

John Clark grew up an all-American boy, son of a machinist in Oklahoma city. He had a paper route and later stocked groceries. In high school he played on the basketball team, but in college he worked in the cafetaria to make a go of it. By sheer application he acquired the only kind of degree a man of service would choose in his day and age—he became an engineer. A series of jobs eventually led to the Corps of Engineers, and from there, through the linkage of friends, he joined a newly formed Office of Energy Analysis within the Department of Commerce. There he applied himself to the development of strategies for containing atomic power plant wastes.

His permanent identity began to breathe more and more easily as the years passed. On a level of which Clark himself was unaware except as a sometimes pensive mood, he began to feel that perhaps he had, by good luck and a strictly virtuous life, escaped the consequences of that other existence.

Then, within three humid, sultry summer weeks, the mysterious magnetism of fate caught him up again in the net he had so striven to escape.

From Hermsberg Mahler had also ascended into paradise upon his death and had raged in impotent fury at his own survival, which went counter to his philosophical convictions and promised yet other miseries in some new life. Hatred impelled him to seek vengeance against *kleiner Helmut* now that vengeance seemed a possibility. The spark of his existence followed an energy storm to the Americas.

His daughter Eva could never forget that brief assault in the reception hall. Despite his crudity and violence, she had sensed a genuine affection deep within the blond SS-guard. He had pointed to experiences Eva longed to have but couldn't achieve in the brief and constrained life that had been left her at that point—rapidly ended after transfer to another camp. She also went to America, now that *he* was there.

The three of them coincided in Washington, D.C., in 1974.

II

CLARK RETURNED to the Department after his customary noon-time walk around the Elipse. On the way he passed the White House and made a jog through Lafayette Park to extend his walk.

It was one of those Washington days—so humid even the eyeballs sweated. Men walked the streets pathetically carrying coats over shoulders, ties loose and pulled down, collars open, mopping brows with soggy handkerchiefs. Tourists stood in long, sweating lines waiting to get into the White House. Cameras hung from their necks and tugging children from their hands. Angry voices shattered the vacation mood.

Clark was made of sterner stuff. He wore his coat about powerful shoulders. His tie was trimly bunched at his neck. He could tough it through southern humidity on pure spirit alone.

A bank sign on Pennsylvania Avenue said that it was 96 degrees. The humidity was hitting eighty. Up ahead the sun blazed down and sparkled in the fountains of Lafayette Park where a few brave lunchers sat on shaded patches of grass while pigeons pranced headbobbing on the walks.

Neither heat nor cold bothered Clark. He went on his walk no matter what. He was as steady as the men of the postal service. Neither hail nor shine nor fear of night—or whatever it said on the face of the postal building. He always walked around the Elipse twice, watching the softball players when they were out, nodding to red-faced, agonized, sweating middle-aged joggers, oggled the White House from a distance, and eventually returned to the Department.

He entered the building from the 14th Street side and glimpsed bearded Jack Hansley up ahead returning from lunch with a tall man who gesticulated with long fingers in an animated manner as he walked. Clark guessed the tall man was yet another of Jack Hansley's school mates, probably another consultant.

When he reached the elevator, those two were already gone, probably taking the stairs to save energy—Hansley was a bit crazy about symbolic gestures.

In his own wing, Clark made a slight detour to pass by Evelyn's office, his throat tightening. He stopped in the door. "Hi," he said, and waved to her. She waved back from an inclined position, elbows on the spread-out Washington Post. She was reading the latest transcripts of the latest tapes. After the wave she looked down again, and Clark reluctantly went to his own office. He munched diet cookies pensively, thinking about her.

Evelyn was the only woman in his office—

discounting the clerical people—and had been hired recently in fulfillment of the Affirmative Action Plan to get the office up to quota on women and minorities.

Unlike Clark she came from the east—Massachussetts. Everything about her spoke of wealth—the slender figure, high cheekbones, the fine white fuzz on her cheeks (you could see it from the right angle in the right light), the softness of her figure, the darkness of her languid eyes, the length of her lashes, the gleam of her pampered hair.

The first time he had come upon her in the office, Clark had almost sucked in his breath—despite the "I Voted for McGovern' button she wore on the knit blouse just above a large, bouncy, braless breast.

He'd nodded to her curtly, had rapidly passed her by. In his office, turned toward the window so that no one would see him do it, he squirted 'Mouthfresh' between his jaws from a thumb-sized aerosol. Then, resolutely, his grey eyes steady in his wide face, one hand self-consciously brushing his crewcut blond hair, he went right back where he'd left her studying a civil rights poster on the bulletin board. He stuck out his hand in the forthright manner of a good midwestern boy.

"Hi," he said. "My name's John Clark. What's yours?"

He had never done anything like that with a woman, neither with a stranger nor a prospective colleague. But Evelyn Bantry aroused a powerful emotion in him, not unlike a memory of long-suppressed desire. He knew her before he knew her, as it were.

We're meant for each other, he'd thought at the time, and he had swallowed at the suddenness, the spontaneous explosion of that thought.

It wasn't possible, not really. She was very, very different from him, quite unlike Betty who worked in Chicago as a nurse and whom Clark more or less meant to marry one of these days.

Evelyn was radical. That soon emerged, and was reinforced, in countless discussions they had with each other. These talks seldom ended on a note of harmony, and yet both of them felt compelled to start them and to prolong them, sometimes even over dinner.

Mostly they talked about work. She had a very different conception of it than he did.

They were in the Energy Game, by Clark's reckoning—providing energy to the American people, American industry. He was in there swinging for the Standard of Living. People like Clark and the work they did ensured a prosperous future.

In Evelyn's eyes this particular section of the Office of Energy Analysis had been created by liberals to balance and check the Atomic Energy Commission's reckless drive for unlimited nuclear power. The section was charged with analysis of nuclear waste containment strategies, and if it was in the Department of Commerce by legal mandate rather than in the AEC, any fool could guess that Congress didn't trust the AEC to do the job right.

Yeah, but . . . Clark's reasoning went somewhat differently. If the atomic power industry couldn't find acceptable ways to manage its wastes, it couldn't expand rapidly enough to provide the American people with the power they demanded, and so, indirectly—

"Screw the American people," Evelyn had cried on one occasion in her liberated way. Clark would still see her as she'd sat, legs up on the corner of her desk, the window behind her flowing hair—red this time. Her naked toes had wiggled angrily in sandals. Clark had stared into the shadows of her loose, bell-bottomed, checkered slacks. In his mind he followed her disappearing leg . . .

Hold that thought—it ain't decent. Evelyn's a nice girl despite her liberation. If she thinks that we're in business to hold up energy consumption, she's wrong, of course, and ought to go to work for the environmental boys. But it's her business, and I hope she stays.

She *was* a nice girl—dammit!

Clark reached up and slapped himself playfully. He had to get her out of his head and get to work. He brushed diet cookie crumbs from the June progress report on the New Mexico siting study. Steadily dropping water tables in that relatively empty state, excellent geology, and a halfway interested Indian tribe all came together as a potential long-term nuclear waste storage site with more than a hundred years of capacity. He opened the report and began to read.

Two floors higher up, bearded Jack Hansley, head of the Office of Energy Analysis, emerged from his carpeted suite with an arm around Ted Aspic's shoulder—an equally young but much taller man.

"It's a far-out idea, Ted," he said. "Way out. But then you've always had far-out notions—and I've always been a sucker for them."

He released Aspic's shoulder and stood for a moment pondering, fingers a-twirl in his beard.

"Tell you what," he resumed with a glance. "I'll take you down to see one of my people—John Clark. He's a bit . . . conservative, shall we say? But a solid man. I've got him doing this kind of stuff—contingency planning. That's about all that the AEC will let us do. See if you can talk him into it. I'll put in a good word for you, of course, but you understand my problem. On an idea like this, I've got to have the staff behind me. By the way, Ted, how come you're into sociology now? Aren't you in physics any more?"

"*Future Now* is into whatever we can get funded," Aspic said. "Just so long as I like the concept." He stepped over to the secretary's desk and picked up a fat brown bag designed to fit beneath an airplane seat.

"Is that what you call it? *Future Now*? How do you like consulting, by the way?"

Aspic's long face drew into a smile. "Freedom, man. It's the freedom trip. Hungry, hustling, but free. No, seriously, we're doing fine. I've got four engineers on board, a couple of economists, a planner, and . . . hold on now—an astrologer!"

"An astrologer. . . ?"

"It's the latest. I'm gambling a bit here, but nowadays . . . Jack, the occult is *in*! Give me another month or two, and I'll have sold my astrologer full time to the Office of Education. I mean it!"

They walked toward the door. Hansley smiled, shaking his head. "Ted," he said, holding the door, "one of these days you'll hit it big. I just know it."

They walked out. The secretary who had been listening with mild interest, picked up her nail polish bottle and slowly, carefully, creamed another layer of turquoise on her left thumb.

Clark seethed inwardly when Hansley left giving an unmistakable signal—*fund this guy!*

He looked down at the card. *Future Now*, Theodore J. Aspic Ill., President. Mountainview, California. A West Coast huckster, to be sure. *"To be sure,"* it echoed in his head, and he saw the puckered lips of a woman on a commercial selling deodorant.

He glanced up at this guy with eyes narrowed in hostility. Something about the man. . . . He was inordinately tall and sat slouched in the chair, his back forming one side of a triangle between the chairback and the seat. His long legs were crossed. He had placed his hands behind his head, long fingers intertwined. Early grey showed at his temples. Large, dark, watery eyes looked across the desk with a measure of hidden merriment, condescension. . . . ? Clark didn't like Ted Aspic one bit. The man had kook written all over him, but he was dangerous kook, well-connected kook.

"Well, sir, what can I do for you, Mr. Aspic?"

"Let's make that Ted, shall we?" The dark eyes

looked at him with moist penetration for a moment. Then Aspic uncoiled his arms and legs and bent down toward his bag. He fumbled around for a moment and came up with a sheaf of Xeroxed sheets. He held the pages in his hand, not looking at them, leaned forward over them.

"Isn't it true that Plutonium-239 has a half-life of 24,000 years?"

Does water flow down hill? Clark thought. He barely nodded.

"And isn't it also true, John, that plutonium wastes have to be contained some 250,000 years? As a consequence of that half-life, I mean?"

"So I have been told," Clark said, hoping the sarcasm would glimmer through.

They were all like this, the well-connected kooks. They discovered atomic wastes one day reading the San Francisco *Chronicle* or the LA *Times*, and then they sailed in here with half-baked notions that a man was supposed to swallow with joy and hallelujas. Had Aspic discovered abandoned salt mines? Would he suggest deep-well injection? Or was it empty missile silos this time? Hansley had dubbed him a physicist, so he probably wanted to shoot the crap up into space at an astronomical cost. On the other hand, this guy looked like a left-wing raddy of the first water. He probably wanted to use the waste to heat black people's pools in winter time or some such nonsense.

I better cool it, Clark told himself. Whatever else this character is, he's the public, and service is the name of the game.

Aspic had been leafing through the pages in his hand. Now he found his place and looked up.

"This is an article I came across recently and it gave me an idea. The Smithsonian Magazine. Article by Dennis Farney."

Clark nodded. He knew the article. It was entitled: "Ominous problem: what to do with radioactive waste." Half the congressional mail lately had dealt with it.

"The part that gave me the idea is this paragraph here on page twenty-four. He's talking about the problem of long-term containment and so on and so forth, and then he says here, 'Some have seriously proposed that society create a new kind of "priesthood" to watch over the waste, much as medieval monks watched over mankind's written history in the Dark Ages. Presumably, this priesthood would have to be supranational in character and somehow insulated from the rise and fall of nations through the centuries.' "

Aspic looked up. Clark regarded him with a steady gaze, but inwardly he groaned. It was much worse than he had thought. Even Congress had passed up *that* paragraph.

"What do you propose to do?"

"I propose to look into the feasibility of setting up such a priesthood. My initial notion was sort of along the lines of the Jesuits, you see, but after we did a bit of work on the back of the envelope, it seemed better to create a hereditary—"

"How much?" Clark asked in a tight little voice.

The dark, watery eyes looked up. "A hundred and fifty kay."

Clark didn't blink; he stared back.

"For phase one," Aspic added.

From the 747's nearly stratospheric altitude, the Rocky Mountains, now flattening slowly toward the west, looked like the uneven scales of a giant brown lizzard. Empty land. . . .

Aspic contemplated the scene below, awash in closely linked thoughts. His long, thin fingers rested lightly on the second gin-over rocks he'd substituted for his usual martinis. The flight was empty and he had three seats all to himself. He'd kicked off his shoes and loosened his tie. He enjoyed now the last hour of that light serenity such trips always gave him. Soon the plane would dip down over the bay and come in for a landing in Francisco. Bronzed, efficient Helen would await him with the kids and tell him all about the tennis games she had or hadn't won. The children would whine and want a souvenir from the airport shops. They'd screech and wail in the wagon all the way home, but Helen wouldn't hear them; she had nerves of steel; and he wouldn't bother to shut them up. Permissive child-rearing . . . no pay-out, no pay-out at all.

He took a sip on the gin and stared down again at the brown emptiness imagining a great monastic cluster down there, a foundation worthy of an ancient Cluny—but devoted to the maintenance of boiling, eternal, atomic wastes. Would the monks chant? Would they evolve a totally new religion over time? Or would one have to invent the religion in advance? A good question that needed exploration, a specific research task to be written into the proposal John Clark had at last, reluctantly, asked be prepared.

Aspic thought about Clark for a second, recall-

ing the man. An upright type, evident even from
the short hair he wore . . . in this day and age.
He'd sat behind his desk upright and stiff. On
the way out Aspic had noted that the man wore
white socks. Had clearly been proud of that
hammerlock-style manly handshake. A typical
privincial kid come to Washington to help run the
great federal machine. Aspic knew how to deal
with them. They were easily flattered into sub-
mission by a show of interest. But Clark. . . .

Clark had aroused in Aspic a kind of hostility
which was far more than merely a mirroring of the
dislike Clark had exuded toward *him*!

Could I have met him somewhere before? Aspic
wondered. Surely not. I've never been in Oshkosh
or Kokomo or Wichita Falls or wherever the hell
he comes from. Maybe in a previous life. . . ?

Aspic smiled to himself, but then the smile
faded and he took a good-sized suck on his drink,
pensively crunched a bit of ice.

A year ago he'd had a stormy love affair with a
lady professor from UCLA during a joint project
from the now defunct National Materials Policy
Commission. She had been the perfect antidote to
Helen—wilting, far-out sensuality. Cheeks a little
saggy. Eyes a little rayed. Long, mournful breasts.
Baggy rears. She'd worn copper bracelots on both
wrists and had been into everything imaginable.

She had introduced him to LSD at the peak of
their romance when he'd spent three, four days in
Los Angeles each week. She believed in reincarnation and swore to him he could retrace his lives
under the sway of acid. He had laughed that off;
she had insisted, quoting Tim Leary, and at last
he'd dropped a little acid on a dare.

Now Aspic pondered that experience.

Inconclusive, by and large. Yet. . . . Amidst all the tortured, ecstatic, twisted, oozing, mind-blowing experiences, he recalled one sequence that had sent him screaming from wall to wall in the bare room they'd used for those sessions. It had been a vision of a concentration camp. Aspic had been a jew, a prominent lawyer reduced to clearing tree-stumps from frozen German earth.

He shuddered at the recall. After that experience he had quietly withdrawn from the professor, had assigned one of the economists to work with her. He'd never touched acid since, would never touch it again.

The stewardess stopped by his seat. "Everything all right?"

He nodded and smiled to her and she moved on.

He lifted and swirled the gin-over-rocks, tempted against all reason to dwell further and deeper on that acid vision, sensing that it contained something important, something that might explain his powerful aversion to John Clark of Commerce.

Aspic took a drink and forced his mind away from the subject. He would discuss the matter with Templar over lunch tomorrow. To Jack Hansley he'd represented Templar as an astrologer, but Cam was much more than that. He was a genuine mystic, little more than a nearsighted kid, but gifted! The kid was *weird!* Making his living casting horoscopes—until Aspic had lifted him up into the middle class by a single wave of his long fingers. Cam might have an explanation. *If* reincarnation really worked, in a manner of speaking (not that it was comparable to a machine, but still) then something might be done with the knowledge, the matter could be explored further with a grant from the National Science Foundation. NSF was an easy mark for such odd things. The results might even be applied in that project with Clark. Heredity. . . .

The pitch of the engines changed ever so slightly. The long descent had begun.

III

A YEAR PASSED before the contract was let. Even
under ordinary circumstances, the federal mills
ground very, very slowly. But in this case other
factors were involved. For one thing, *Future Now*
received a non-competed procurement which required long justifications. For another, Clark went
into the job with a great deal less than his usual
enthusiasm. Only periodic prods from the front
office made him move the papers toward the inevitable dump of a hundred and fifty thousand
dollars in Aspic's direction. And, most impor-
tantly, during this time Clark was preoccupied
with Evelyn Bantry.

He was especially preoccupied with her on this
Friday morning; so much so that he could barely
keep his mind on the substance of the meeting.

Clark represented Commerce on an inter-
agency working group. The first meeting of the
group was in progress in a windowless AEC conference room— a large table ringed by a grey wall
of bureaucratic faces. A man from the Bureau of

Indian Affairs held forth acrimoniously against the New Mexico Plan, hitting the table with a fist and pointing index. His point, which he made in as many ways as he could think of and as often as he could grab the word, was that the decision of the Shashtuk Tribal Council was in no way binding on the Department—by which he meant *his* department, Interior. AEC and Commerce should be lauded for finding a long-term storage site, but they could place it somewhere other than on BIA land, thank you.

Ordinarily Clark would have been roused to battle-ardor by such bureaucratic attack. Today he couldn't focus, nor did he have to. Interior would lose this battle. Energy came first. And tonight he'd score, by God! Finally, at long, long last, he'd *score!*

His mind wandered into the future with anticipation. Too many hours still separated him from the inevitable. At eleven he had a meeting with Aspic—progress report time. Then a quick walk around the Elipse. Clark doubted that he'd get much work done in the afternoon, excited as he was, so he'd do some reading, maybe, and cut out early, and buy the wine she'd asked him to bring, and a bunch of flowers, get showered and shaved, and then at six sharp he'd be in front of her apartment door on New Hampshire Avenue for home-cooked dinner and . . . you know what!

Man . . .

Clark glanced at his watch. Quarter to eleven. He had to get out of here. Rising, he excused himself, pleading another appointment. He gathered papers into his briefcase and left.

In a year his appearance had changed. Now his

blond hair hung down long and rich—George Washington, Tom Jefferson style. He sported a good-sized mustache with down-curling ends. He wore a natty checkered suit and dark socks under buckled shoes. His briefcase was imitation crocodile.

On the way out he stopped briefly before a large bulletin board and searched the sheaves of position descriptions for a GS-14. Not that he needed the money. But if he married Evelyn, he should be a grade higher in case she wanted to quit working and have babies. He saw two or three 14's advertised, but they were all in far-off places. Nobody would grab those, of course. He passed on.

He met Aspic on the way in, in the dark entry hall of Commerce, and they went up to the office together. At the moment Clark could even take Aspic without irritation. He almost bantered with the tall man on the way. They settled down—Clark behind his desk, Aspic in front of it.

"You want the door closed?" Aspic asked with a sly grin.

Aspic knew how much this project embarrassed Clark. The men in the office had begun to call him the 'plutonium priest,' and 'Father,' and 'Brother Clark.' But now Clark's humor was excellent.

"Naw," he said, waving a hand, "leave it open."

They got down to business.

Aspic's original idea had grown with time into a veritable forest of concepts. He spread before Clark a long flow-diagram depicting the study phases, a maze of rectangles connected by lines. His long index finger pointed to boxes as he explained the sequence of tasks. The psycho-

profile questionnaires to determine the optimal
personality mix of various gradations of a Permanent Priesthood were in testing now, with good
results. Ceremonial and Ritualistics were not yet
scoped out fully, but Cam Templar—whom Clark
had met on the last trip, if he could recall—had
started work.

"But what worries me," Aspic said, leaning
over the desk, tapping a large box in which, tenta-
tively, someone had drawn a question mark in
pencil, lightly, "is Succession Insurance."

His long form straightened and he sat down in
his chair.

"My thinking is this way, John. For a century or
two we might rely on natural recruitment. Or we
could make the priesthood heridITary, with
everyone living right in the monastic compound,
and cross-breeding between monasteries—that's
Option B, as you'll recall. But I just can't give you
any certainty beyond about four generations. So
much could change in that time. The social fabric
might break down—it almost did under Nixon. It
could happen again—and, who knows, next time
we might not make it. No matter how appealing or
frightening or whatever we make the religion
inside, sooner or later people might start to drift
from the priesthood, enticed away by the outside.
Look at the Catholics, a perfect analogy. We've got
to come up with . . . something. Something
really hard to bind these people to the Custodial
Service. Now I've got some ideas along those
lines, and NSF had given us a little grant to help
explore it, but in the long run it might take big
money."

Aspic looked at Clark wondering if he had said

too much already. If the Permanent Priesthood concept made Clark shy, what Aspic now had in mind would make him bolt! But he had to lay some foundations now—it was either that or talk Jack Hansley into appointing another project officer.

Clark's eyes had narrowed and he had straightened up behind his desk. "What are you talking about?"

"Ohhh," Aspic said. He looked down at his hands. He chose his words with care. More than ever he was certain that this man across the desk had played a crucial role in his, in Aspic's life. Discounting for genetic differences, which inevitably prevented identical *appearance*, Clark nevertheless incarnated that certain *personality*. Aspic knew from an LSD vision. He had returned to that vision under Cam Templar's careful tutelage. He saw the German SS-guard in Clark, the cruel blond beast with ready boots and rifle stock. It was in his eyes, the manner, even in the fall of the man's long hair—(whatever had induced him to let it grow long?)—as if the man's soul-force radiated out through the physical matrix forcing it to give a semblance of identity even in the external. Such a man was dangerous, had to be watched, would have to be caught, would taste retribution.

Aspic unfolded his hands, looked up. "Ohh," he said again, "it's nothing much really, just an extension of the principle of heredity into another dimension, as it were. I'm not really ready to discuss it in detail—"

"Say, Johnny, about that wine I asked you to bri—"

She stood in the doorway at the conclusion of a quick run down the hall, just a touch breathless, red hair flowing, braless breasts heaving, golden rings around her arm.

"Evelyn! Evelyn Bantry, for God's sake!"

"Teddy!"

They embraced affectionately and then looked at each other at arm's length. Clark watched with a fist-sized hole in his stomach.

"Harvard Square? Sixty nine?" he asked.

"Has it been that long?" she asked. "Teddy, what a pleasant surprise! Are you . . ." she glanced at Clark. "I mean—is this business?"

Aspic nodded. "But you. You wouldn't be working here, by any chance?"

"Sure," she said, "This is my turf, Ted. And you? Are you on your own? Or still with—was it GE?"

"Free as a bird," he said. "On my own. I've formed this small consulting group on the West Coast—but say, Evelyn. This is no place. What about lunch? Can you make it?"

"Why not," she said impulsively with a darting glance at Clark. "Let's catch up on things on my time—rather than Uncle's." She turned to Clark. "Sorry to barge in on a meeting like this, John. Your door was open and so I. . . ." Her head went back to Aspic. "Just pick me up at my office down the hall." She gestured. "Bye, now."

"Evelyn!" Clark called, but she had already disappeared.

At five ten minute intervals Clark trudged out of his office and went down the hall past hers. Two o'clock, two-fifteen, two-twenty, quarter to three.

He began to call her apartment. At first there
was no answer. Then the phone was busy. Finally
an operator told him it was out of order.

At four o'clock he went home without a word to
anyone. In the closet-sized kitchen of his efficiency apartment, he rummaged in the back of a
cabinet until he came up with a pint of whiskey,
three-quarters full. Slouched in the single
armchair in the living room, he drank the booze
out of the bottle slowly, staring at his watch from
time to time. At five-thirty he straightened his tie,
dabbed at his mustache, brushed his hair, and
went down into the street. He bought a bottle of
wine in a liquor store down the block. He hailed a
cab and told it to take him to 20th and New Hampshire Avenue.

He walked through the gold-carpeted lobby,
passed beneath the chandelier, nodded to the
guard in his red, epauletted uniform. His finger
touched the elevator button and the device turned
a faint pink. Silvery doors slid aside. He stepped
in and found Floor Nine. The elevator surged up.

Before her door he pressed the bell, later ham-
mered on the imitation oak with his fist. At last
she opened the door a crack, dishelved, in a robe.
He pushed his way in, went past her through
a short, narrow hall. In the dining nook he
glimpsed the table—probably set the night before—a rich table cloth, two plates, silver, crystal,
unlit candles, a flowery centerpiece.

Evelyn came behind him, talking, but he didn't
hear what she said. Blood pounded in his temples, behind his eyes, sang in his ears. He had
never been inside her place, but he found the
bedroom without trouble. Aspic lay on the bed,

naked but for shorts, an apprehensive look on his face as he stared up at Clark framed in the door. The Princess-style push-button phone on the dresser was off the hook and made a rythmic, cricket noise.

For a second Clark stared at Aspic and at the bed. The covers had been pushed off the greyish, much-used, wrinkled bed sheet. Her clothes lay in a heap to one side, hastily dropped.

"Hey . . ." Aspic called, seeing the look in Clark's eyes, regretting now the laughs he and Ev had had about Clark between bouts of passion. He extended a hand toward Clark in a warding, cajoling gesture.

Clark took the bottle by its neck and threw it at Aspic with all of his force. But he was unsteady and slow from drinking. Aspic saw the motion and rolled out of the way. The bottle hit the soft, padded back-board of the bed and fell unharmed on the sheet, a dark-green, round-bellied Portugese rose.

A sob formed in Clark's throat. He didn't have his heart in the act of violence. Evelyn! She had destroyed him, but he could do nothing to her. He turned aside and brushed past her without a look.

She had followed him to the bedroom door and stood with her arms raised protectively in front, tiny fists beneath her chin, eyes shrinking. Four martinis, it echoed in her mind while her eyes were on Clark. Four martinis, she told herself dully, suddenly sobered and aghast at her own stupidity. She had been dazed and utterly silly and now . . . She felt sick to her stomach and turned away.

Clark stopped in the dinette, suppressing sobs.

He took hold of the fine, patterned damask. A jerk sent plates, silver, crystal, candles, and flower-piece crashing to the terazzo floor. He walked out of the apartment toward the elevator.

Back in his own apartment, Clark went to the only piece of furniture he owned in this furnished efficiency—an old-fashioned rolltop desk. He began to rummage in its narrow cubicles. Can-celled checks, plastic name tags he'd worn at con-ferences, an insurance policy, letters from Mom, a yellow-red garage bill, a little black book! He took it with him to the bedroom, sat down on the bed, and lifted the telephone onto his lap. He dialed a string of numbers.

Far away, in the Windy City, on the shores of Lake Michigan, a telephone rang, and rang, and rang. Then at last, just as he was about to hang up in despair, a cheery voice came on.

"Hello?"

"Betty!" he husked into the mouthpiece. "Oh, Betty, I love you, I love you."

IV

In the fall of 2006, they finished building the odd-shaped radar dishes on top of the hexagonal building some distance from the compound, and three days later planes started to land scientific teams at the government airport a couple of kilometers beyond Perpetual, New Mexico.

Radar dishes?

John Clark had no other name for them. Oh, sure. They probably had fancy-dancy names and did something unusual, else there wouldn't be tight security surrounding the project. But to him they looked like radar dishes.

He gunned the jeep and roared past the new complex oggling those shallow baskets of wire, reddened now in the setting sun. He suspected that this was a defense installation after all and had nothing to do with rad-waste storage. Probably some of that super-hush psycho stuff rumored to be under development now that the U.S. was about to plunge into the Russo-Chinese war despite Hubbard's election-year promises. The

Chinese, supposedly, had missiles implanted
with living human brains so cleverly trained they
could evade virtually any kind of mechanical
counter-rocket. Psycho was the only answer.
From what Clark had picked up, it projected fields
of the greatest sensitivity and caused schizoid
reactions in the missile-brains leading to their
self-chosen destruction high up in the atmosphere.

God, he hoped Hubbard would stay the hell out
of that war. He personally didn't care. He was too
old for that sort of thing by a long shot. But the
boys. . . .

No. He for one didn't see any reason for a
Russo-Chinese intervention, yet tonight on the
news three cabinet officials in speeches across the
country, had floated up the first trial baloon. In
other words, the decision had already been made.

Desert streaked by on either side of him, lovely
in the gathering dark. It had rained briefly two
days ago—the first time this year—and the desert
had bloomed like a woman in love. Clark was of
two minds about rain. On the one hand it made
this country beautiful beyond compare. On the
other it caused trouble. The torrent had revealed
several leaks into articaverns G and K, and Emergency had been mobilized for two days and a
night to plug the leaks, lest steam formation
generate pressures great enough to cause a series
of cave-ins. God; what a mess that'd be!

Up ahead Clark saw the dirt road and applied
pressure to the brake. He turned the jeep off to the
right and bounced forward leaving a trail of dust.
Chief Walk-on-air would see that cloud and know
that old man Clark was coming—although the

chief didn't need outward signs to know the future, he knew it, although you couldn't get him to say much more than a handful of words at a time. Walk-on-air had told him about those leaks, but without the rain they hadn't been able to find them.

Clark felt revulsion. He hated rad-waste with a depth and passion so basic it was kind of Super-loathing. Years and years and years ago he had gladly grabbed a GS-14 to get the hell out of Washington, to marry Betty, and to live among decent folk far from the pointyheads and whores of the Potomac. It had been a good life at first. Betty had turned out to be his kind of girl—calm, handy, and true as true-blue could be. Later on, when the New Mexico Plan came to fruition—his plan—he had volunteered to help set up the site among the Shashtuk indians. In those days there had been nothing out here but cactus and earth huts. They'd lived in a trailer for two years. Things sure had changed since then. Look at Perpetual: ten thousand people. A rail-line brought the rad-waste from thousands of miles away— kilometers, Clark; don't always forget about metrication. Four great compounds. Ninety-six arti-caverns. And yet it was all like ashes in the mouth.

Clark couldn't recall precisely when it had hit him. Before the Act, of course. Perhaps in the late eighties, eighty-four, eighty-six . . . therabouts in time. He'd already felt it sharply in eighty-seven, the year they broke inflation's back and the civil service took a sixty-percent paycut. Freddy was nine years old, Gerry seven. That same year they passed the Nuclear Waste Security Act, and people like Clark were frozen in their jobs, willy-

nilly. They had no power, the handful of guys out
in the field running these hazardous waste de-
pots. The Union had bargained away their future
for a whopping pension plan. A few people had
muttered about 20th century serfs in the media,
but the Kansas salt mine disaster had blinded
everyone. Besides, Clark could have left the service had he wanted to—a free man still. But who
would do that with depression raging out there
and two young boys to feed. So he had stayed, but
that feeling had grown by degrees.

He still remembered sitting at the kitchen table,
nights, his fist around a can of beer, morose, staring at the placemat left over from dinner, the TV
going in another room, thinking about Aspic,
wondering if Aspic had been behind the Nuclear
Waste Security Act, the first shot in a war planned
long ago. But it didn't seem likely. He'd lost sight
of all those people. Aspic had been a kook. Some-
body had probably found him out.

Betty came up behind him and put her hands on
his shoulder by his neck. He could feel her lips
touch the top of his head. The short bristles
tickled.

"Don't brood, honey."

But he had brooded on and on until it was too
late.

Up ahead loomed a Shashtuk roundhouse.
Smoke curled from its center. A '95 Chevy sedan
stood parked off to the side. It had been doctored
Indian style with roof cut off by hack-saw. Dogs
came yelping and then, recognizing his scent,
turned into tail-wobbling welcome.

He alighted with a groan, heaving his big belly.
Got to diet. Just Gotto! He went into the hut, bend-

ing to clear the low door. Dung-smoke and Shashtuk odors mingled in his nostrils. An ancient crone squatted by the fire with a pan. A young boy sat on a cot.

"Hya, Superintendent."

Clark nodded to the boy. "Where's the chief?"

The boy gestured into darkness.

"Up on the rise?" Clark asked.

The boy nodded.

Clark went out again and trekked slowly up the slight elevation behind the house, marked by two large cacti resembling hands stretched to the sky. The dogs followed him a short distance, then dropped back.

He found Chief Walk-on-air seated between the giant plants, hands on his knees, his face turned to the west where the sun had finally set and only a thin line of crimson separated darkness from darkness. The old man had a wrinkled indian face and jet-black hair bound into a braid in the back. His eyes were closed.

Clark caught his breath a bit and then sat down on the bare ground. Doing so he noticed a bundle next to the chief. Had Walk-on-air been out collecting peyote? Or was he bound outward now? In the darkness Clark couldn't see whether the bag was full or not. It was just a blackness on the ground.

Clark waited knowing that no amount of coaxing would make the old chief speak until he chose to do so on his own accord. Clark wasn't any younger than the indian; perhaps he was even older. But in all other respects the chief was the teacher, Clark the disciple.

It had all begun fifteen years ago when Clark

had heard about the old man's prophetic powers and had sought him out with a question: "Will I ever leave Perpetual and get a start in another kind of business?"

Clark still didn't have an answer to that question. But from the first moment of their meeting, he had been attracted to the chief, almost indifferently at first, had acquiesced in a kind of strange relationship. It consisted of weekly meetings filled with long silences broken occasionally by a deep rumble of words. In the third year Walk-on-air announced abruptly that he had "hunted" Clark's spirit, had caught it, and found it good. In those days Clark had not yet learned his lesson and had pressed the chief to explain himself—but to no avail. But some weeks later the indian had fed him some peyote cut into small slices, and chewing them Clark had been catapulted into paradise. Then, twice a year thereafter, less frequently some years, the chief had repeated that procedure.

His visionary experiences didn't change Clark outwardly. He continued on, the same as he was, but he no longer asked his questions, having been satisfied on that account in some mysterious way. He knew that he would live and die here in Perpetual, that it was meet and fitting, that somehow it was meant to be, had something to do with his old longing to serve the public.

Clark had resigned himself to that. But he hated it. God, he hated it. The chief was his only real consolation—the chief and the annual communion with the Holy Mushroom, an experience he kept from Betty with as much jealous secrecy as his humiliation by one Evelyn Bantry, whose

memory still sometimes returned to him, whose
figure appeared in his peyote visions, many-faced
but always the same.

Across the bit of rock-strewn dirt, Chief Walk-
on-air opened his eyes.

"Good-bye old friend," the indian rumbled in a
gutteral, hard tone.

Good-bye? Clark sat still, didn't answer. He'd
let the chief say what he had to say. Questions
only dammed up the thin trickle of communications that came out of the old man.

Old man. . . . I'm an old man too!

"The Big Sky will come and fetch away Walk-
on-air."

Silence. The crimson line on the horizon had
thinned out and had disappeared. Now the cacti
were like shadows. The first stars had appeared
and blinked in rising heat.

"This is a bad place for dying. Walk-on-air
going south. Far away."

Why? Why is this a bad place for dying?

They sat in silence for a long, long time. Then
the chief stirred again.

"White man has a spirit-catcher. Very evil
machine. Walk-on-air go south, die, come back to
Shashtuk land."

"What do you mean, spirit-catcher," Clark
blurted out. He slapped a hand to his mouth, but it
was too late. He had disrupted the flow.

For a long, long time he waited, but nothing
more would come from the indian. The sky slowly
thickened with stars, the Milky Way dusted
across his vision when he lifted his head. At last
Clark rose.

"Good-bye, old Chief," he said, and he walked back down toward the jeep.

On the way home he had a bad moment. Suddenly he felt in the pit of his stomach a kind of burning pressure he hadn't felt in years now, an unpleasant echo of the late eighties when he'd gone through inner hell. He couldn't well imagine that Walk-on-air would actually leave. He was as much a part of Clark's life as—as Betty was, as the arti-caverns with their vats of eternally bubbling hi-rad sludges. The old man—old man, indeed! He was as strong as a bull. Not a thread of silver in his hair. He must have been joking. He was off peyote hunting deep in Mexico. He did that every year. The bag had looked very flat on the ground next to the indian. He'd be back in a couple of weeks, and then Clark would go out to see him again on Wednesday nights as usual. Nonsense about dying, spirit-catchers, stuff like that.

He felt a little better.

Soon he wheeled the jeep onto the surfaced road, gunned it and roared homeward. Betty and he lived inside the compound in the superintendent's mansion that seemed so cavernously large now that the children were gone. When Gerry had visited earlier this summer bringing his whole family with him—all five children whose names Clark hadn't been able to keep straight—they had fitted in with lots of room to spare. After he and Betty had waved good-bye and the big red bus had pulled away, they'd walked back in and the place had echoes like a tomb.

Near the compound Clark noticed that lights

still burned in the newfangled hexagonal security complex. He slowed down and peered inside through the tall barbed wire fence with its outreaching arms. As he watched he saw a man walk past a window, and he caught his breath involuntarily, thinking he'd seen Ted Aspic—or at any rate an old man with snow-white hair who might have been Aspic if Aspic still lived. Clark stomped on the brakes. Wheezing, he got out and leaned against the jeep, arms folded across his heavy beer-gut. He watched the window with a face as stiff as a board. The engine idled at his back. But nothing more happened.

Clark shook his head. He was seeing things. He got back into the jeep and drove on. Guards waved him through. He drove between gigantic silver storage tanks that held the low-rad waste and up toward the artificial hill where the super's mansion stood with its lead-insulated walls.

On the kitchen table Betty had left out a glass of milk and a couple of cookies. He looked at the snack, but then changed his mind. He didn't feel so good in the stomach.

Two weeks passed but the chief hadn't returned. Three weeks. Five weeks. Toward the end, just before he was hospitalized in Perpetual, Clark had driven to the indian's roundhouse every night, although the pain in his gut had forced him to drive doubled-up and Betty had begged him tearfully to relent, to give up, to be at peace, to find consolation in the Twenty-third Psalm—which she held out to him, marked with a red ribbon. . . .

"The Lord is my shepherd, I shall not want . . .

he maketh me to lie down in green pastures . . .
yea, though I walk through the valley of the
shadow of death. . . ."

Finally the ambulance came. Attendants took
him from the jeep where he crouched in agonies
against the wheel. Lights flashed and the sirens
wailed. But they sounded far away, as if meant for
another.

He lingered on for two weeks more, now up,
now down.

In this time he had lucid moments when an
easing of his pain and the diminishing action of
the drugs they fed him coincided. Food came to
him through a tube in his arm. He had lost most of
his stomach to cancer; the doctors couldn't understand why he hadn't complained before.

In his states of temporary bliss, he listened to
the talk that buzzed around him. The USA had
entered the Russo-Chinese war with a brigade of
intervention that grew to several armies within
several days. Brain-missiles had been dispatched
from China aimed at West Coast cities, but a new
defensive system had neutralized them over the
Pacific. People repeated stories about windstorm
damage and tidal waves—consequences of those
H-explosions. Then Betty came and chewed back
her tears as she held his hand. Good old Betty.
Then, one time, nurses gossiped bitchily at the
foot of his bed about that new security complex
near the compound, saying it was a regular
whorehouse, with people paid to make love in
there on Friday nights. Inwardly Clark smiled. He
knew what went on in that hexagonal building. It
was a hush-hush psycho-station, set up here to
prevent Chink bombing of those cursed, damned,

boiling vats . . . Well, he'd soon be free of all that
and go where you went when it was all said and
done. Then, one time, he thought he saw Aspic
hovering over the bed in company of a short, bald
man who wore thick rimless glasses and seemed
familiar to Clark. It was a fantasy, of course, but
nevertheless Clark forgave Aspic everything. No
point in holding grudges, not any more. Death
dissolves everything. And finally they stood by
his bed—Frederick and Gerald, his stalwart sons.
One of them wore a uniform. Clark tried to nod to
them, to encourage them, but he couldn't move
his head.

That night he died and went up into paradise.

"Fantastic," Aspic said, and by his side Cam
Templar nodded.

They stood before a wall completely filled with
tiny rectangles, each one closed off by thick,
curved panelettes of glass. Minute bits of light
glowed inside some of these miniature aquaria,
one flame per cubicle—but these lights weren't
fish and they didn't swim in water. They were
souls suspended in super-cooled nitrogen and
held by subtle magnetic fields.

Aspic saw his own image reflected from the
curved glass panes, a little bent and very much
diminished by the small surfaces. Age sat on him
lightly—at least judging by appearances. His hair
was completely white by now, but it hadn't
thinned at all. His long face was powerfully
tanned and gave him a youngish look accented
with thin white rayings of maturity around the
eyes and a kind of tightness about the skin. While

ther people wrinkled in old age, his skin appeared to shrink, giving him a haggard look.

He wished he felt as young as he appeared, but he didn't. Now, in this moment of completion, he wondered about the cost of all this—not the money cost, of course. The Feds had provided most of that. But the psychic cost lay on him heavily—all those meetings, all those lunches, all those favors rendered, all that talk, all those trips to Washington, a thousand Congressional hearings, ten thousand backroom discussions.

A new light blinked on and drew Aspic's attention. Almost immediately a telephone rang somewhere. Templar moved off to answer it. The time was early morning and in this part of the complex all the clerical help had retired many hours ago. He watched Templar from the back, a short, old little man. Templar was eight years his junior but looked fifteen years older—white of complexion, fading, nearly blind despite those heavy lenses. After a moment Templar came back.

He pointed to the rectangle that had just lit up, nodded. "That's him," he said.

Aspic watched the micro-flame. He was thinking about motives.

All around him sprawled this complex, the first of its kind in the world, the only one of its kind. Its evolution and development had taken three decades, some of the best physicists in the world, a tremendous amount of public money, and all of Aspic's persuasive powers. It worked. It was the culmination of a life of labor. And yet it was just the first step. Many such centers would be built in time. The Perpetual Priesthood would rise from

these centers, would be replenished through their
mediations—provided, of course, that the god-
damned war didn't stop progress altogether. The
war had come at the worst possible time. From
now on a man wouldn't get a hearing in
Washington about domestic programs. Best to lie
low, in fact, lest someone discover how much this
facility cost to run and the kind of talent it
employed. The budget cutters would have a ball
despite AEC protests. Lie low. Take a vacation.

Yes, he'd take off, get away from all this. The job
was done. The motive that had started this ball
rolling had been satisfied. It burned there, that
tiny little thing. Clark, or whatever was left of the
man. He had triggered the idea, he and some acid
memories of a concentration camp. And now
Clark sat in his own little prison. He glimmered in
there, longing to incarnate, tortured by desire,
sensing the copulations of the entire region in the
air . . . but he couldn't dissolve himself in flesh,
he'd have to hang there suspended between two
existences—a spiritual terror of unspeakable
menace, according to Templar. Templar knew
these things.

Sooner or later, Aspic told himself, it was
bound to happen. Sooner or later someone was
bound to learn to control soul energies. And we
did it. Cam and I!

Nothing mysterious, really; just the same old
physics in another guise, just the same old
mathematics oriented to another dimension.

Not that they knew much about it, Aspic reflected. They had found the tip of the iceberg.
They knew how to hold the souls and how to
condition them to some extent. When it was all

over, Clark, or whatever was left of Clark, would have a powerful compulsion to stay near radiation wastes. He'd have an abiding love for the stuff. He'd worship it. He'd feel possessive about it. He'd seek it out wherever it occurred. His senses would guide him to it.

Or that, at any rate, had been the outcome of some experiments with short-lived fruit flies. You couldn't generalize too much, of course.

"How long have these been incubating," Aspic asked, sweeping the wall with a gesture. Thirty little flames burned behind glass. Not counting Clark, all the deaths had occurred within a fifty-mile radius, the range of the magnets. They were all sexually screened, all of them souls with masculine tendencies.

"It varies," Templar said. "The oldest ones are two weeks old."

"So tomorrow. . . ?"

"Tomorrow we'll incarnate them. We've got another batch of volunteers assembled, so it should go smoothly."

"Las Vegas tourists again?"

"Mostly," Templar answered, "although we've had to reach farther out this time. The war. . . ."

"That damned war!" Aspic exploded. He reached up and rubbed his eyes with long, slender fingers. After a moment he turned to Templar.

"Tell you what, Cam. Now that we've got Clark on ice, I think I'll take a nice long vacation. Don't do anything with him until I get back. I need some relaxation. These last few months. . . ."

He clicked his tongue and shook his head. "I think I'll head south. Mexico City, Caracas, maybe Santiago. Thank God the war is still a northern phenomenon. Meantime we'll just let Johnny stew. It's the least I can do for him." He grinned suddenly.

"Don't overdo it," Templar warned. He took off his rimless glasses and polished them with a handkerchief. "We don't know how long these little pulses last." He inclined his head toward the tiny votive candles behind glass. Then he looked at Aspic, his eyes a little out of focus. "For all we know, they might go out."

"So?" Aspic said. His dark, watery eyes were cold. Then he continued in a changed tone. "They don't go out. None of the experimentals ever did. Whatever those little things are, they're tenacious." He reached out and touched Templar on the shoulder. "I know what bothers you, old man. It's the torture. You've got a bleeding heart, my friend. Well, let me tell you something—"

But Aspic interrupted himself. He wouldn't talk about *that* any more. It seemed a little odd to hark back to an experience that he, Theodore Aspic, had never really had.

"I'm not criticizing, Ted. Just . . . don't overdo it."

"All right, all right," Aspic said a little irritably, holding up his hands. "Let's get someone to put Clark on conditioning and call it a night."

Four weeks later Aspic drove toward Mexico City from a suburban estate in a rented Cadillac. He sat in the back with two young things he had hired for the duration, and now they were giggling messing inside his fly while the chauffeur drove behind a pane of glass. The headlight beams lifted squat, thick trees out of the on-rushing murk.

Aspic sighed. He felt the old excitement, but it was entirely in his head. Down below nothing responded. He reached for the spaker. "Faster," he said, "Faster, faster." The chauffeur increased the flow of gas.

Aspic leaned back, closed his eyes. He conjured up memories of women he had possessed, went back and lingered on details. But it wouldn't work tonight. He was too tired, the party had been a bore, he'd drunk a bit too much.

He opened his eyes just in time to see an ancient indian step out onto the road from behind a tree. Instinctively the driver jerked the car to the left . . . too far . . . back again. Tires screamed in some kind of terror. Everything went up and down and sideways and lights and glass and still-ness and dripping ozzing wind moved grass next to Aspic's face.

V

CLARK—WHO WAS NO LONGER Clark but someone else—had to wait until his new brain had developed, until he had learned to walk and talk and all those things. And even then he had to hide his curiosity so that his parents and playmates wouldn't think him weird. By age three he secretly read old books that had chanced into the hands of these backwoods people. By age four he discovered at last which century this was. Chance had brought a town circular into his hands at the May fair, and he noted with great wonder that it was the 23rd century, midway through the 23rd, 2256 to be exact.

How time doth fly. . . .

Let's see now, he said to himself. I've been there 250 years, which is something of a record, I'd guess, considering that most souls don't last more than a month in paradise, maximally speaking.

He didn't confide his discoveries to anyone. He bided his time out there with the herds on the mutagrass prairie. At age fifteen he ran away from home, old enough and strong enough to fend for

himself. As for experience, he possessed that of
ten life times.

His current name was Tankers Jack. His father's
name was Justins Tanker. They had called his
father Portos Justin . . . and so on and so forth.
His mother's name was Tankers Two and people
called her Twodie. She was younger than Tankers
One and older than Tankers Three, and she ran
away at age thirty-five and became Wallies
Oneish. Wally was a mutant and couldn't be
choosy.

For reasons he still couldn't entirely com-
prehend (birth had disoriented him slightly), he
had selected for himself a slender, longish body
with sensitive digits and large, dark, moist eyes.
He took after Twodie rather than Justins Tanker, a
large, bony man who never spoke except with fist
and boot but could toss a lasso with the finesse of a
20th century conductor urging *pianissimo*.

Jack knew all these people—from *way* back.

His father had been his grandson in 18th century Turkey. His mother had been his husband in
revolutionary France—although at that time Jack
had been a Jaqueline. Others in the village also
belonged to his circle. He had been drawn down
to them—to Betty, who was the Healer's ageing
mother and who'd soon make the passage again;
to Freddy, his son, who'd surfaced as his brother;
and yet others he had known, closely or remotely,
in many pasts. He recognized them instantly
given his third eye—an invisible 'eye,' to be sure,
not one of those mutant aberrations.

But he hadn't seen Evelyn anywhere, and above
all he longed to see her. He knew he'd see Walk-

on-air again. Besides it didn't matter. Walk-on-air was everywhere.

He arrived in Perpetual, New Mexico five years older and much wiser about the 23rd century.

He came in by what was left of the ancient road, a young man with a flashing eye, black hair. He wore a tall, round hat with a stiff, wide rim. His legs and lower body were wrapped in long strips of rough, grey cotton tied at intervals with leather bands. His trunk was covered by a woven blanket with a hole in the center for his head. Around his shoulder hung a carrysack and from his left ear a golden ring.

He walked toward Plutonium, a tiny figure next to a monstrous construction that now occupied the site of the compound: a proud monastic fortress of tremendous pods and walls and parapets, circled with moats of steaming atomic lava, drawbridges over the moats, pennants on the pod-tips, and a bright glitter of prayer ribbons in the wind. Crowds of pilgrims waited for entry next to one of the bridges, and Jack saw people from all corners of the region. He saw monks in twentieth century garb, a shockingly nostalgic sight amidst this primitive but powerful architecture. In twenty years Jack had become accustomed to cowls, jerkins, wrap-me-ups, and—if you were rich and a townsman—embroidered, ankle-length coats.

Perpetual itself, five or six kemits beyond Plutonium was the carry-cow flew, was 'perpetual' in name alone, for nothing had remained the same except a bit of the layout. A city wall ringed the place, but not as massive or as well maintained as he'd seen elsewhere on his travels. Perpetual needed no protection, not with the monastery nearby.

He stopped at the very first inn he came to, the House of the Nucleon, complete with a hand-painted sign out front showing little flames moving in a spiral.

This being afternoon and the place empty, the proprietor himself took an interest in Jack, served him a foaming mug of warmish beer and talked about Plutonium, his elbows on the bar.

The place was unique, the proprietor said. No other monastic foundation like it existed anywhere on earth, the man said, setting Jack to musing.

By "earth" Jack knew the man to mean the continental United States, the North American *land*, for the institutional thing had passed away in the wake of the Russo-Chinese Intervention, soon after the brain-missiles of all the nations had learned to communicate telepathically and had conspired to bring the whole damn rotting mess down in one glorious Armaggedon. Well, they had both failed and succeeded. The old world had suddenly passed away. But Man had survived and began to fill up all the spots again. Too bad for the Old Order. It had been much more varied and rich than this primitive culture of towns, herdsmen, farmers, and brigands. But Jack couldn't blame the brains, not really. What is a man to do when he can sense and think and feel and desire—and has a missile for a body?

He returned his attention to the Inn's proprietor who, in the twentieth century, would have been urged to try Scope. The man was telling him about the marvellous power of Plutonium to attract disciples. The life up there was hard and dangerous. They didn't touch women and lived in narrow cells just barely wide enough to let a man lie down. Many of them died from strange and mysterious sores. It was known all over Shashtuk country and well beyond. Yet young men came from all over, about Jack's age, usually, and they had a burning desire for that life up there. "God is great," the proprietor said, bowing his bald head rimmed by black hair.

Then he looked up and asked Jack if he was one of them.

"I might be," Jack answered with a smile.

"Those who are, know!" the man said seriously.

Jack made a note to remember that when he approached Plutonium's masters. He recalled the compulsion-creating conditioning process of his early days of spirit incarceration. But what compulsion had been wiped away by the existential terrors he had experienced during months of suspension between two lives, the very experience ancient catholics must have had in mind by the fires of purgatory. He had been purged, all right. His energy identity had been forced to contemplate itself, hour after hour, through what seemed a handful of eternities. He'd come to memorize his past, to imprint it indelibly on his deepest awareness. Then someone had released him at last. But instead of incarnating with alacrity, Jack had careened off into the very stratospheres of paradise seeking recovery from his tortures. Fearless now, he had plunged into the very center of the white disc of light and there, abiding in healing solitude, he had seemed to be in company of Walk-on-air. By the time he emerged to incarnate again, quietly, deliberately, one quarter of a millenium had passed away below.

He took a swig of beer, wiped his mouth with the back of his hand, and said: "I have no money, innkeeper, but I'm a scribe."

"Welcome, welcome," the man said, bowing. "Feel at home, Tankers Jack. I'll pass out the word and you'll be drowned in business. The last scribe came by more than a year ago."

The proprietor rubbed his hands with pleasure. Such luck to snag a scribe. His house would be full for weeks. He led Jack personally to the very best room in the house, lovely with its blue-white wallpaper obtained at great expense from a travelling merchant. The bed—a double mattress; three pillows; and thick, fluffy Harvey pelts for cover against night-chill.

Another significant change between that time and this, Jack noted, his eye on the milk-white pelts of the rare, disappearing giant rabbit. The sun seldom peeked through the overhead murk; volcanic ash and sediment circled up there around and around the globe. It would take centuries to restore illumination to its ancient maximum. It was cold in New Mexico, even in June.

He waited until the proprietor had left. Gazing after the man, it occurred to him that the bald, fellow might be Cam Templar, Aspic's astrologer, but he couldn't be sure, having only met Templar once, long ago, in Washington, D.C. If it was Templar, he had certainly come down in the world, karma-wise. The man's head disappeared down the stairs, and Jack closed the door.

He took binoculars from his carry-sack—he'd found the instrument in the never-used bomb-shelter of a destroyed estate far to the north, where the ice starts. He walked to the window. He lifted the binoculars toward Plutonium on the horizon and searched the monastery's silhouette until he spied, barely visible, six baskets of wire high up between the pods. Passing by the massive complex, he hadn't been able to see them. But they were there.

Once upon a time he had thought them radar dishes.

After four days of reading and writing letters—hundreds of letters—Jack decided to take a holiday. His earnings had been good, the people generous. They liked the way he dramatized the messages from relatives far and wide, the way his eyes twinkled when he read funny things and the way his voice choked up when he catalogued woes.

The Innkeeper hired four extra grils to keep the beer and the meat flowing, but all too often he caught them dreamily admiring the scribe from the edge of the perpetual circle of people around him. He also suspected that they slipped into his room at night for more substantial samples of his passion—but the Innkeeper need not have worred or envied, whichever it was. Jack waited for one girl and only one. He thought he'd earned her affection at last, and the mysterious forces of cosmic magnetism would sooner or later sweep her into his path.

He borrowed a horse from the Innkeeper's stable and rode away in an ancient direction toward nightfall. He had chosen a Wednesday night for this venture—for old times' sake.

The horse plodded forward wearily, its heavy head going up and down, tired from dragging shaped concrete slabs all day from a nearby gorge overpass ruined ages ago but serving now as a kind of quarry. In its place now hung a spidery ropeboard thing, a graceful curve above the abyss.

Up above the moon was a diffusion of light in an atmosphere loaded with suspended particles. Down below the ground was far more lush, a swaying grass-scape, a rolling prairie of muta-grass.

In place of the upright cacti Jack found a willow with its hair hanging low. Near the tree sat Walk-on-air, an ancient, wrinkled indian with jet-black hair pulled into a braid in the back. His eyes were closed. He sat facing the spot where the setting sun had caused a dirty brown line of light be-tween sky and ground.

Jack dismounted and sat down near the chief to wait.

After a while the chief opened one eye. It twin-kled merrily, its white a little yellow. He opened the other eye and broke into a huge grin.

"Hello, old friend."

"Hello, Chief Walk-on-air."

"You've done right well for yourself," the chief said, gesturing toward Jack. "A nice combination you've concocted. A bit of the gypsy in you, a bit of the hero, nice and slender but strong in the wrist and the arm; your eyes are very expressive, and the nose hints a little at carnivorous birds. That golden earring gives you a mysterious air, the lips are sensuous to the right degree. The hair is straight, yet at the ends, it has a kind of graceful curl. No doubt you're an accomplished singer, swordsman, and story-teller too, can read men's palms and see the future in goblets of dark wine. Am I right?"

"You know everything, Chief Walk-on-air."

"On the contrary, Tankers Jack—a kind of racy name, that, I must say. No, no, my friend. I wallow in blissful ignorance. She's always unfolding, always unfolding like a flower that forever germinates into the future. There is no end to her mysteries."

"Who is she?"

"The Cosmic Flower, the Absolute Change."

"I thought there was nothing beyond you, Chief."

The indian laughed, his head thrown back. He was thoroughly amused. He chortled and chuckled.

"Tankers Jack," he said at last, wiping his eye, "you're an incorrigible Barbarian. You've been inside the brilliant light—yet you returned to earth. For what? A woman. Right?"

"You have all the answers, Chief."

"Listen to me, old friend. Do you know what happens to people who go into that brilliant light when it appears in paradise? People who don't get frightened and don't shy away toward the red of the spectrum?"

"I don't, Chief."

"They become angels, Tankers Jack. They go up into higher lives. They turn into planets and suns. But you—you come back for a woman. And then you ask me whether there is anything beyond me. I also worship a woman. There is always something beyond. Otherwise we'd all curl up and die."

Jack's horse blew air through its nostrils with a low blurb and stamped a leg.

"Since I have, as you say, thrown away a chance at angelic existence," Jack said, "let me turn to petty practicalities. When will I see her?"

Chief Walk-on-air laughed. "What's the hurry, Jack? You've waited three hundred years or more. What's a decade or two or even a life or two."

"Chief," Jack said tensely, nearly rising from his cross-legged position, "don't you tease me. I couldn't possibly wait decades—much less lives!"

Chief Walk-on-air chortled, blubbled. Tears ran down his wrinkled cheeks. He pointed a gnarled finger. "Look at you," he said, "just look at you. I can't get over it. Here you are, all got up to kill, a hearth-throb. My God, Jack, how do you keep the ladies from your bed? But when I see you, I see old Clark sitting there like a pile of misery, his beer-gut coming out to *here!* Oh, Spirits, oh, Flower!"

"When?" Jack demanded crossly. He felt totally at ease with Walk-on-air. They had shared an eternity together in the brilliance.

"All right, all right," the chief said. "How can a god refuse anything to a mortal like you." He narrowed his eyes half mockingly. "The time is ripe. It'll happen soon. But there is still a wee-little-bitty bad karma clinging to you, Tankers Jack. You haven't scraped away quite all of it. Those spirit-catchers are still up there—and you're responsible for them. A word to the wise. . . .?"

"And then?"

"And then the nefarious and strange ways of
the Lady Flower will guide you in magical ways
into her presence," the chief pronounced. "After
that it'll be up to you, of course. I can't guarantee a
thing. I wallow in blissful ignorance. I sit here and
wait for the next marvel that may drop from her
hand."

"Why here?" Jack demanded. "And why sitting? Why don't you wander about like I do. You
see more things that way."

"Because," the chief said, and he grinned
broadly, "because you're just a young god and I'm
an old one. One or two stories a millennium are
quite sufficient for me. The doctor tells me not to
get too excited, you know. If I overdo it, I might
become an angel."

With that the chief threw back his head and
laughed most merrily.

VI

THE SIREN SHRIEKED and echoed through the intricately laid corridors of Central Pod. It called upon the brotherhood to rise. Plutonium's day had begun.

Jack awoke with a start and almost sat up straight. He remembered himself in time and, accustomed to the maneuver by now, he slid from his vault-like chamber feet first. He landed in the corridor and reached for his clothing. Monks dressed on all sides of him, slipping into jeans, shirts, sweaters, or sweat shirts—the obligatory uniform of the monastery.

It was Jack's fifteenth day in Plutonium.

He had arrived, had slipped into the monastery almost without notice, just another novice, just another compulsive come to seek satisfaction at the bosom of God. He had come, but he had not yet conquered.

This day, the fifteenth, would roll by like the others. And then would come another, and then another. The ordinary mortal, Jack told himself, would long have lost his patience with all this and told his precious karma to go hang, but he was not an ordinary man and so he stayed on, waiting for his opportunity.

He dressed, like the others, and took an inventory of his situation.

Many levels above him, sealed off by guards, was what the monks called The Mystery. Many levels below him, in the ancient arti-caverns, the members of the Hierarchy would now be preparing for the one and only ceremony of the day. A few levels above them, at ground level, others of the Hierarchy would be cutting bread into small pieces for the breakfast that would follow, a humble, monastic meal. A hundred kermits to the south of here, a monkish caravan would be loading tents and setting the missile into motion again. The missle, so he understood, rested on two long carts tied end to end, and the carts were drawn by sixteen oxen. The missile, presumably, would be chattering in its mad way.

That described his situation fairly concisely.

He finished dressing and wondered how long it would take for sixteen oxen to cover a hundred kermits. Ten days? Twenty days? He hoped it was ten days at most. Even a man with the patience of Job would want to escape this lunatic complex—especially if a girl awaited somewhere in the future beyond the moats of Plutonium.

Jack joined other monks and walked along the corridor toward spiralling stairs that led to the depths beneath the complex. This corridor, like those in most buildings nowadays, coiled unpredictably through the building. The total darkness was eased only by ancient phosphorescent paint, delivered here ages ago for disposal, which these latter-day guardians of radiation had smeared liberally on the walls. The paint bathed corridor and monks in an errie, greenish light.

The missile bothered Jack in more ways than one. On the one hand, he might be counting on it far too much. On the other, it *was* a missile. The brain in it was still alive, and if the brain lived its other parts might still be functional. It was a legacy from the twentieth century, a token affection sent down through time. He couldn't even start to guess how the brain had survived. Few mechanical objects had escaped the ravages of time. Cars were heaps of rust, batteries dead, ballpoints dry. Only Aspic's Mystery still ran, that much was evident—and this nuclear bomb lifted by sweepers from a lake in what had been Texas. They had made those babies to endure, Jack reflected. They probably ran off solar energy with a sealed-in life-support system to maintain the brain-mass, a super-duper stainless steel ecology—and now it jabbered nonsense through an amplifier attached to its underside. Take that back. It didn't chatter nonsense all the time. From time to time it pleaded with its finders to drop it from a mountain onto rocks. When it was sane, it wished to die, in other words. When sanity left it, it spoke about Armageddon, a woman named Hester, and a child called Tom.

What *hath* God wrought!

Jack reached the stairs and went down, hands on the railing. His mind continued to turn around the missile.

Word of the thing had come three days ago. Excited messengers had burst into Plutonium with the good news. A group of sweepers had discovered a Godbod larger than any found heretofore. On top of that, this Godbod had a voice and said odd things—prophecies, some of the messengers claimed; others, more sober or less imaginative, said it merely spouted old gibberish. Jack had gone to interview all the messengers he could find, and with some reluctance had concluded that the thing was a brain-missile all right. Now, going down around and around the spiral staircase, he wondered if he had miscalculated the effect it would have.

News of this Godbod had sent waves of shock through Plutonium. Most of the ordinary monks lived in total idleness. They neither spun or wove. The first hour of the day was structured by the ceremony. Thereafter, unless a man belonged to the Hierarchy, he could spend his time any way he wished. Plutonium by day or night was a savage battlefield of roaming gangs. Battle-sounds could be heard throughout the complex, cries, blows, running feet, the heavy breathing of men. The victors usually raped the youngest of the vanquished. Such would be the fifteenth day, such had been the first, the second, and all the rest—with one exception.

On the day when the messengers had arrived, Plutonium had buzzed like a hive stirred by a stick. News of a talking Godbod had put a stop to the usual amusements of the brotherhood. Men had gathered in excited clumps, discussing the event, and groups had formed spontaneously to plan the reception. Jack had concluded that such excitement would be magnified many times when the missile actually arrived, and while the brothers swarmed out to greet this new find, he hoped to be upstairs, communing with the Mystery. He hoped, at least, that security upstairs would be greatly relaxed. Otherwise, as he had discovered, it would be nearly impossible to approach Aspic's satanic machine.

But what if they didn't relax the guard? What then?

From down below Jack could hear the roar of voices. The monks gathered in Cavern B, as it had been called in the old days, the largest of the storage areas. By the time Jack reached the place, the cavern had filled up with monks, a huge assembly, a sea of heads moving and humming. Above them he could see, in the distance, the abbot and several ministrants preparing for the ceremony. Baskets of hot rocks stood on the platform, and ministrants arranged themselves beside them. The abbot, wearing asbestos gloves, placed a silvery canister centrally on the altar. Torches stuck into holders mounted on the wall behind him threw the only light in the cavernous, echoing room. Their flames reflected on rows of vats on either side. Hot sludges boiled and bubbled inside those giant pots, just starting on the first leg of that 250,000 year journey toward ionic exhaustion.

The abbot raised his hands high into the air. A hush fell on the monks. The best part of their day would now begin. After the chanting and the reading were over, the ministrants would bring the baskets through the throng. Each monk would take a rock. Ceremony called for a ritual kiss followed by a touch of forehead, throat, navel, and gonads with the rocks. Most of the monks went well beyond this requirement. They hugged them over their bodies. Contact with the rocks, which had been exposed to high-level radiation, satisfied some deep need in these miserable men.

Jack noted his own position and moved to his right, toward the wall. In the center of the throng, the ministrants would certainly pass closely by him, and he tried to avoid what all the rest had come to enjoy—exposure to the radiation. He felt a surge of pity for the monks. He couldn't help them. They had been conditioned, once and for all; their bodies needed something biology knew nothing about. But future generations had to be protected from this obscene slavery. Jack wondered briefly whether it was really true—that he, himself, by a series of rash acts in concentration camp, had set in motion the horror he witnessed on every hand: these savage men covered with sores and lesions. Could one man, with one act, leave such a legacy of trauma?

The abbot started chanting in a reedy voice, and an ocean of voices answered him, a deep, male lowing that rose and fell. Jack looked up and watched the altar. From his new perspective by the wall, in uncomfortable proximity to one of the vats, he could now see a large group of monks on the platform. They were sweepers awaiting the abbot's blessing before setting out. Each carried a small box, sack, or bottle. Discovery of the missile had put new vigor into sweeping. Now everyone was eager to find a Godbod even more magnificent than the talking needle.

Jack eyed the sweepers on the platform. Sweepers had been his first encounter with Plutonium. He had seen them in all parts of the country during his wanderings, wretched creatures combing the countryside, sniffing for radiation as they went, trusting their compulsions to lead them to the holy stuff wherever it was, however, deep or however high, yes, even on the bottom of lakes. They carried bits of hot stuff with them. Without those bits of inoculation, compulsions drove them back to Plutonium. He had seen them huddled beside ancient freeways in miserable camps; he had seen them begging food, standing in the middle of village streets, and he had seen women throwing them bread from a safe distance. The common people understood Plutonium in their way. They knew that sickness followed the monks. They hurried them along, out of the hamlet, away from the cattle. Holy sickness, to be sure. But move along, please.

The chant died out in a final, multitonal hum, beautiful in its way—would have been beautiful had Jack not known the unholy desire that gave it such feeling. Across the distance from the altar now came the abbot's voice, reading the scriptures. The echoing hall swallowed some of the words, but Jack knew what the abbot was saying. He spoke about Gods ineffable presence in the room. He blessed this Holy Interface where divinity was operative. He spoke of vigilance and of the evil world without, where Godbod's holy emanations didn't reach. The words were lame, without much cadence. A contractor's anlayst had written the text trying to beat a deadline, no doubt. But neither scriptures nor dogma mattered much, Jack knew. The real faith burned in the monks' entrails—an implanted compulsion. The software didn't play a role so long as the hardware worked.

When your innards wrench and tear you, you don't need much of a theology.

Jack could feel the growing excitement. Greedy eyes devoured the baskets from a distance. The reading would be over soon. Jack slipped away, between two vats, and sought the deeper darkness of a recess in the wall. He pressed into it and felt, against his back, heavy studs that, in the old days, had held the radiation shields in place. They had been removed, of course. From this vantage point he could glimpse, between the vats the progress of the ceremony, the pathetic antics of the monks, the vigilance of ministrants.

Theft of an irradiated rock was considered a capital offense. Once a day, and once a day *only*, were monks allowed to feel the particles— granted, of course, that the whole hive was hot, up to the very last pennant cracking in the wind above the highest pod.

The ministrants came down and then moved back, collecting the rocks as they went. Jack faded back into the crowd and watched the abbot lift on high the shining canister in a final blessing. Then he turned and blessed the sweepers, whereupon a ministrant approached them and handed over bits of Godbod for their boxes, sacks and bottles.

The ceremony was over, but the monks stood their guard, not a man moving. It was like this every morning. They felt the Lord's peace in the cavern. They didn't want to leave. The vats threw out emanations, and they gloried in the feeling. But enough was enough. The ministrants now turned policemen and began to press the crowd toward the exit carrying clubs in their hands. Jack felt a surge of hunger. He went out and up the stairs toward the eating halls.

Jack sat on a bench against the wall next to some monks he knew. These men were of the pious sort, a small percentage of Plutonium's population, simple creatures who took the doctrine seriously, shunned gangs, and spent their days in little prayer chambers strewn about the complex reading the scriptures hung from the wall by chains. Jack had associated himself with these men. His piercing look and a regal manner he had assumed had protected him from violence and rape. He put about also that he was a Hierarchy spy, which helped. But he found it best, like any other beast of the jungle, to fade into a herd of others to fend off predators. These men were the least offensive of all those in the hive.

Jack munched his piece of bread and a single carrot. He turned to the man on his left, a whispy creature by name of Johns Jim.

"Jim," he said, "any news about the Prophet?" ("Prophet" was one name for the new discovery, "needle" another.)

"I don't know," Jim said. "You should have better information." He whispered: "You're with the Hierarchy. But I feel it," he continued in a normal voice. He pointed to his stomach. "I feel it here. It's coming closer."

"How many days do you think it'll take?" Jack asked.

Jim didn't have a chance to answer. At that moment a man burst into the room to their right and ran between benches toward the only table in the hall, to their left, where the abbot sat taking his breakfast flanked by high officials of Plutonium.

The man was tall, haggard and, although he wore dark clothing, it was evident immediately that he was blood-stained. His eyes shone with a kind of craze.

He arrived at the abbot's table and leaned across it without the customary handshake which, no longer used as a form of greeting in the twenty-third century, was still an obligatory courtesy in Plutonium.

Jack saw the man whispering to the abbot, and then the abbot fell back in his chair as if he had sustained a blow. In a second he, in turn, whispered into the ear of his chief aide who, in his turn, gave evidence of shocked dismay.

The two men rose and gestured to the leadership. Then, in a body, the whole group left, taking the haggard man along.

This brief scene caused unusual excitement in the brotherhood. The monks occupied several halls the size of this one, strung out end to end in a circle along the girth of Central Pod. The word spread quickly through all the rooms, and in minutes excited groups had formed, discussing, speculating. Men were sent running to check with their contacts in the Hierarchy. To Jack it seemed like a replay of the scene some days ago when the missile's discovery had been announced.

A half hour later—the monks were still milling in the eating hall—the word finally filtered out. Johns Jim, who had run off to consult with the deputy assistant theologian, a friend of his, brought back news to Jack's group. His thin, grey face was long as he approached, his mouth half open in the anticipation of speech.

"They stole it," he called before even reaching his group. "They got it. They're all dead. It's gone."

The pious monks enclosed him in a circle. Then, in fits and starts, the story came out. A large armed party of unknown affiliation had attacked the triumphant caravan bringing the needle home. The monkish escort had been slaughtered. I alone am escaped to tell thee. That, in essence, had been the haggard man's story. The world had intervened and stolen Godbod, Plutonium's most cherished capture in a hundred years.

Jack cursed inwardly at the news. He saw his plans for action foiled. No missile, no excitement. No thronging mass would leave Plutonium to meet the double-car and the sixteen oxen. His face, like that of the others, turned long and sad, but his sadness came from another source.

Then, in an eye-wink, the situation changed abruptly.

Movements in Plutonium were coordinated with a siren, a hand-cranked affair. It announced the morning service and also feeding times at noon and in the evening. In fifteen days Jack had heard only a single siren, a very unpleasant sound, but tolerable. Now, slicing through the air toward him came the sound of several sirens, all operating at a different pitch. The sound was so piercing he involuntarily covered his ears and bent his head. This was a new phenomenon. He divined at once that it was an emergency call. He had judged correctly. The monks around were electrified into motion. They ran for the exits and crashed through them, nearly trampling one another. The eating hall was suddenly empty. Only Jack stood against the wall, his eyes on a sea of wooden benches.

The sirens stopped as suddenly as they had started, and now he could hear the thunder of feet descending stairs. The floor of the hall trembled slightly from multiple impacts.

He waited until the sound had died down. Then, with cool resolution, he turned and went the other way, up toward the roof of Central Pod. He knew that his chance had come at last. The waiting was over, and he could act.

He saw no one on the stairs going up. No one in the corridors that led toward the Mystery. Jack couldn't believe it, but it was true. He had been prepared to deal with opposition if he had to. Ten lifetimes had taught him many murderious arts. But there was no need. When all the sirens were let loose to wail through Plutonium like desert ghouls gone mad, all men were called from their posts, apparently, even those above, those who had blocked his access in days past.

He walked freely into the restricted area. He stood before a door. On the other side of it he heard a faint hum, a hum he hadn't heard in this era. He looked to right and left. Still no one around. His hand depressed the handle. The door opened a crack, then more, then all the way. He stepped in.

Consoles stood around the room—a room that had been moved intact, from the ancient security complex to the top of Plutonium by God knew what exertions or when. Here electrical lights,

presumably fed from nuclear reactors made to
last, glowed dimly overhead. The floor was plastic. Bright metal gleamed everywhere. Against
one wall scores of tiny flames glowed behind
glass panelettes. They gave Jack a nauseous pulse
of remembrance.

His eyes a little wild, he looked about and found
what he needed, a large polished rock used as a
paperweight on a desk. He took the stone and
went toward the panels. He hesitated before setting to work. He was about to destroy a strange,
unique technology, perhaps Western Man's last
great breakthrough. It might never be invented
again. It would be a loss to Science, the science of
some future. But his hesitation was brief. Tiny
flames flickered before him, souls in transition,
karmic fires. He took a deep breath and began to
free them, one by one. Broken glass fell at his feet
and cold gas hissed around his hands, covering
his arm with artificial rime.

VII

Discovery of the savage destruction went through Plutonium like another great convulsion. By that time Jack had long disappeared into the country, clad like a scribe again, humming a tune, longing for Evelyn, and glad that the missile was lost somewhere to the south. For that reason, he went north. Monks were sent out to capture the criminals, but they found only pious ladies bringing baskets of alms and simple pilgrims in their tents. The Hierarchy, meanwhile, met again to ponder alternatives.

They were horror-struck and knew themselves mortally wounded. The Mystery, and it alone, replenished the priestly ranks. It was the heart of the cult. They tended the machinery with loving care. In ample store rooms thoughtfully filled by Old Order founders, they could always find the part needed to keep the panel lights green. Most often a wafer failed; sometimes a wire had to be replaced; more rarely a gas canister would run dry

nd a full one had to be snapped in its place. The
Iierarchy had calculated that five centuries could
pass before the warehouses were empty.

But now they saw the Mystery in the paroxysm
of death. It smoked amidst a wreckage of metal
and glass. A storm had passed through the
warehouse. A fire still raged in one end of it,
filling the space with poison fumes. The cult
would surely die—especially if some upstart
group had a Godbod that spoke strange
prophecies.

After some days of agonized consultation, the
abbot decided to mount an armed excursion—to
recover Godbod; the Mystery was beyond help.
Plutonium organized for war. The monkish army,
ten thousand men or more, each carrying a bit of
Godbod, led by the haggard messenger, moved
south to the scene of the crime. Here investiga-
tions were ordered, and after some days the army
wheeled north. It picked up the cold trail of the
thieves.

The trail was difficult to follow. The leader of
the enemy, a man described as short, blond,
sturdy, wide-faced, and steady, had not been recognized by anyone in the area. He had come out of
nowhere, he and his men. People guessed he was
a war chief attached to a city. They inferred this
from the discipline of the men he led, the quality
of the cloth they wore, and the system they had
devised to move the giant needle toward the
north.

The leader had abandoned the carts and the
oxen. His men had placed the needle into a large
net suspended between twenty-four horses,
twelve on each side. Soldiers rode the leading and

trailing animals on right and left. This method of transport was faster than the one the monks had used. The group travelled off the beaten paths Plutojacks had to seek reports of them. Few had seen the odd if memorable group, a swiftly moving, silent band—silent but for the silver needle in its hammock which, by all reports, continuously spouted gibberish.

As the monkish army moved, it lived off the land. Discipline was difficult to enforce. The population in its path grew fearful and mounted resistance. But slowly, like a radiating locust hered, Plutonium groped its way north.

The leader of the thieves was Alans Shepherd.

In his twelfth existence he had accumulated much merit by a life of service in the cause of justice, the culmination of a long series of evolutions to ever higher vibrational spheres. But in his thirteenth incarnation, as a physicist in what was then the United States (of fading memory), he had indulged a passion for vengeance and had loaded himself with heavy karmic debt.

In a succession of lives since then, brief and violent lives they were, he had sunk ever lower, unable to stop his downward drift, until this time, in his Shephered incarnation, darkness enveloped his awareness to a significant extent, and only bits and pieces of earlier light came through the chinks of his moral obscurity.

One of those bits of light, though he didn't know it, emanated from his chief and sovereign, Zeronica, once his daughter and once his mistress, and other things besides in a long existence that went back to the Crusades.

She alone, of all the folk he knew, aroused in him a dim memory of something higher, and he had served her now for several years, doggishly loyal, uncharacteristically mild.

Returning now with his prize of prizes, he gave himself a little hope, just a tiny bit of hope, that she would reward his loyalty at last. With this final act, he would make her foremost among the leaders of the world. Now he would deserve the reward she had promised him, years ago, in the shadow of the ice. If she refused him this time, he didn't know *what* he would do.

Spurred by such motives, he drove his men to great exertions, and the group reached Phoenix long before the plutojacks had even organized for systematic pursuit. He entered the city gates at night, in secrecy. His men slipped the Godbod into the dungeons beneath the Presidential Pod. She came to see it that same night, a cloak about her night dress. Godbod was sleeping at the time and she couldn't question it. Messengers had told her about the miraculous voice. Her manner, as always, was aloof and cool, and Shepherd went to bed that night with the bitter taste of disappointment in his throat. He tried to console himself saying he was a man of power and influence second to none in Phoenix. But the thought gave him no solace. In her presence he was still a bandit, and though he never let the thought flit across the surface of his mind, he knew that her eyes ruled his, now as ever. He tossed and turned on his lonely bed. She hadn't even greeted him. Her first words had bit his soul deeply, opening wounds. "I don't know," she had said down in the dungeon amidst torch flickers that echoed back from the dull gleam of Godbod's hull. "Is this *all*?" she had asked. "It's just a piece of metal, isn't it?"

She herself had demanded of him year after year, for three years at the least, that he should capture for Phoenix the one thing it lacked. Now that he had done it, she called it a piece of metal.

The next day she had a sitting basket hung from the ceiling in the dungeon. She sat beside the needle and tried to hold a conversation with the awakened spirit within. This went on for two days. Then she sent for Shephered and discharged her frustrations into his steady face, angered by Godbod's incomprehensibilities.

"You should've let the plutos have him," she said to Shepherd at the end, her voice dripping with contempt. "He, he—" She gestured at the needle, slapping the air with a hand slack at the wrist. "This is no god, Shepherd! Can't be. Maybe it's just one of those talking machines the old books tell about."

Back in his own quarters, Shepherd kicked the mutants. He stayed within for three days, drinking. He recalled his carefree life beneath the ice and cursed his fate.

Two weeks later the war caught up with Tankers Jack.

Rumors had preceded it and had already set him to wondering. He was staying in a small village when plutojacks over-ran the hamlet. Jack escaped the worst of the killing. He knew the code words of the priesthood. He mingled with the band as it departed, pretending to be a sweeper and out of touch with Plutonium. His appearance aroused no great concern. Most of the priests wore modern clothing acquired along the way.

Deep in the heart of a forest in what had been a desert in Clark's day, around a smoky fire, Jack learned that God himself had destroyed the Mystery, angry at the priesthood's lack of vigilance. Later, as the fire fell to ashes and the monks lay back to sleep, an old priest by name of Goosers Texas, who had eyed Jack with interest, looked about, beckoned with a grizzled head and a squinting eye. When Jack sat down beside him, the old man said:

"You look like an intelligent man, Tankers Jack. You'll go far in the priesthood. You say that you were on a sweep when all this happened. And these simpletons told you the story we of the Hierarchy have put about. Well, you deserve better, Tankers Jack. The truth is, God did nothing to the Mystery. A man destroyed it."

The old eyes searched for a reaction, and Jack opened his eyes in astonishment.

"Yes," said the priest, nodding toward the fire. "Yes, by the Holy Interface, we know, we of the Hierarchy."

Jack signalled his respect and said that secret knowledge belonged by rights to those who carried the burdens of responsibility.

The old priest nodded and sighed. "Yes," he said, "the burdens are heavy." He leaned closer and whispered: "The abbot told me—"

"The *abbot*?!" Jack breathed.

"Yes, sir," said the priest. He nodded gravely. He picked up a stick, leaned forward with a groan, and threw it into the fading embers, evoking sparks. He sank back again.

"The abbot points to the Woman of the North."

The monk nodded to himself. "She did it—her henchmen stole the needle."

Jack grew alert. A woman had been mentioned—a woman tied karmically to Plutonium.

He told the priest that, pardon his ignorance, but he had never heard about the Woman of the North. What was the story?

"Well," said the priest, "I reckon you must have been sweeping far to the east of here. And you mustn't have been around these parts for a good many years—am I right?"

Jack allowed that Goosers Texas was right on the button.

The dry stick burst into a flame. The old man leaned forward and held his hands toward the heat to warm them. When he resumed, his tone had changed. He would be telling a story.

"Well," he said, his old face red and gashed by moving shadows, "her name is Zeronica. An odd name, I'm sure you'll grant. The presidents of Phoenix all called themselves Henry until the male line died out. Henrys Henry, each and every one of them. She was the daughter and only child of One-eyed Henry, as the people called him, the last of the Henries. Nothing wrong with his eyes, you understand. But he squinted a lot, sort of like this."

The old man turned and squinted with one eye. His features grew lewd. The open eye glinted oddly, as if with a smile. Jack had the uncanny sensation that he was sitting beside Walk-on-air.

"He called her Henrys Oneish in the customary way," the old man resumed. "He knew she would never be any man's Twodie. She was a President's daughter, after all. But that wasn't good enough for the Woman of the North. After one-eyed Henry died, she changed her name in a ceremony in Phoenix Square, right in front of the Presidential Pod. She even sent out runners to advertise the fact. They explained what her name meant. She didn't want anyone to miss the meaning. At first the people smiled at this. They figured she would marry the man the Phoenix Congress selected as president, that being the natural expectation. But she had another notion.

"The people of Phoenix eat out of her hand, you understand. But there are those, even some in Phoenix, who blame her father for her ways. Henry never had a son. He spent his nights in a harem of those feathery creatures people call Dingbats around that part of the country. Zeronica was more or less an accident, I understand, or else his wife had taken a lover. However that may have been, once Zeronica was up and about, Henry took a shine to her and brought her up as if she'd been his son. He taught her reading and writing and got her ancient books to read. He even sent her on a tour of the world, and that's where it happened, years before her father died."

The old man stopped and refuelled the fire again. Its flames drew from the darkness the shape of pines bunched closely together.

"Somewhere far in the northeast, up where the ice starts," he went on, "a band of bandits captured Zeronica during that tour. Henry had sent her with an escort, of course, a hundred men, I think. But Zeronica had quarrelled with the captain of her guard, and one morning, without his knowledge, she rode off early with just her tutor to keep her company. That's when she met Alans Shepherd, the man who helped her later.

"The story has it that this Shepherd—by reputation a violent man, famous for harrassing the caravan route that snakes along at ice-edge—well, he killed the tutor and dragged Zeronica off to his tent. She bounced limply on the rump of his horse, unconscious in her furs, knocked on the head with a club. Shepherd yelled and screamed with joy, savage that he is. But once he got her inside the tent and swabbed her back to waking, she got the upper hand in a hurry. The story has it that she stopped him with a look in her eye. That's the kind she is. And before you know it, Shepherd was yelling through a tent-flap. Slaves came running with food and drink. She sat on a hassock like a first lady. He behaved like she was an equal. And the two of them made a deal.

"What the deal was came out later. The story goes that she agreed to become his Oneish after it was over, after her power was secured. She promised him she'd make him president. She would be his only wife. And, sure enough, people say, Alans Shepherd went to her chamber in the presidential pod after Congress swore her in as president-person. And he said to her, 'Zeronica,' he said, 'we have an agreement. You promised to marry me after I put you in power. I have put you in power, so be as good as your word.'

"I don't know for a certainty that he used those words, Tankers Jack, or exactly what happened," the old man said after a pause. "There are many stories. Maybe he tried to embrace her too, as he had once tried to do in his tent—and I guess you

can imagine him pressing her against a credenza
or a table, trying to find her lips with his. But
whichever way it was, whether she slapped him
as some say, or whether she slipped from his
grasp, quick as a weasel, or whether they never
came within a sem of each other, all stories agree
that she said to him, pointing at him: "You put me
in power, Shepherd? You?" And then she started
laughing and laughed and laughed. Her head
went way back. And she doubled over and
slapped her thighs. And Shepherd, who thought
he was a very big man because people feared his
men, why, he couldn't stand her laughter. He took
his hat and walked out of there. He swore to his
closest companions that he'd replace the bitch,
chase her out of Phoenix and take over himself.
But he never did. He is still there, working for her,
and Phoenix has only one president-person, and
that's Zeronica. People say Shepherd still loves
her, still hopes, and can't do her harm.

"Well, soon after that, Zeronica started making
changes, and—"

"How did she gain power?" Jack interrupted.

"What? Oh, that. Well, she brought Shephered
and his ruffians back with her from her world
tour. Shepherd followed her like a little thin dog,
and his pack right behind him. She called them
her personal body guard. One-eyed Henry chuckled at it fondly. He let her do anything she
pleased. Slowly Shepherd built up his forces. He
hired the scum of Phoenix, people without cult or
property. By the time Henry died, Shepherd's
gang was larger than the Phoenix military. But
people didn't know that until the scum came from
the cracks in the clay. Members of Congress who

opposed her election learned to fear Shepherd's raiders. One or two pods burned down mysteriously. A couple of members died in tavern brawls. The upshot was that they elected Zeronica president-person and no questions asked."

The old man leaned forward, groaned a little, and tossed more wood on the fire. He shivered a little. His years made him cold. He sank back at last, his eyes pensive and far away. He was finished for the moment.

"Well?" Jack prompted. He felt a great excitement in his bones.

"Well," said the old man with a sign, "she's a witch, I tell you. It's those books, I suspect, or the old ruins she saw on her travels—God knows I've seen my share of them; never could make much out of such rat havens; but her mind was charged up with reading. At any rate, she called in Congress soon after she took over and she proclaimed that here—I mean Phoenix now, you understand—that here in Phoenix they would establish the New Secular Order. That's what she called it. She told them how the old world would come back. God had decreed that it would happen. That came from a book too, I think. Her reasoning was that it would happen in Phoenix, and nowhere else, because there had been a prophecy about a bird, and the bird had been called Phoenix, and when it burned it rose up again from the ashes.

"On the feast of Superstar, which some cults celebrate in the month of December—two years ago, it was—Zeronica made a declaration freeing all the mutants in Phoenix and on the surrounding lands, saying that slavery was evil and didn't fit the New Secular Order. She said she saw no difference between mutants and men. See what I mean? Well, Congress voted its support for her and Shepherd put down the rebellion on the farms.

"Then, last year—the girl's quite handy with proclamations, Tankers Jack," the old man said, shaking his head, "she announced that women were equal to men—"

"She said *that!*" cried Tankers Jack.

"She did," nodded the monk.

"And she got away with it?"

"She did," said the monk again. "I don't rightly know why, either. But, as I said, she's a witch and people eat out of her hand. They believe her. I've heard a story or two to the effect that she has assembled all sorts of ancient mysteries and has a priesthood of her own, trying to make them work. She has no decency, you see, and scorns the customs. Among those things, or so I am told, she has a mystery that makes pictures on the wall. You can see people walking and hear them talk as if they were real. And with this magic she bamboozles the Congress to do things her way. The New Secular Order!" the old man spat. "God forbid such heresey. . . .

"And so, Tankers Jack," he concluded, "I think the abbot is right when he suspects her. It wouldn't surprise the Hierarchy to learn that Alans Shepherd led the thieves that killed our brothers. But don't say a word to these simple yokels," he said, gesturing all about. "They don't need to know what we know. But you'll go a long ways in the order, Tankers Jack. You need to hear the truth. But now wrap up and go to sleep. The cold is deepening."

The old man pulled a blanket about himself. He lay down, his back to the fire. His eyes closed and he seemed to go to sleep.

Jack sat erect for a long time. He stared into the smallish flame licking the last piece of wood. Ash lay on the log like reptile scale; the flame burned blue above the glow of embers.

He saw Walk-on-air's fine hand in all this—the meeting with Goosers Texas, the story of Zeronica. He recognized her touch across the ages and knew her though he'd never seen her current form. Fateful, all this. He had to hurry away into the growing night chill from this spot of fading warmth. His karmic journey was not quite over. She too, like he, attracted Plutonium. And so did Alan Shepherd, the unknown third in this star-crossed party, whose pathetic quest for Zeronica's love seemed oddly reminiscent of something lost in Long Ago. A missile had found her. Jack had to find it. He owed as much to the twentieth century.

VIII

THE MISSILE GLOWED very high up, suspended nose down in the center of a wooden tower. The tower stood in Phoenix Square. The Square stood in the center of Phoenix. And Phoenix was the center of the world. Bright stones spelling an inscription said so.

Jack stood at the foot of the tower and peered up into the height. Darkness gathered as the sun set, but its filtered rays made the missile's hull glow red. It might have been a brass bell hung in a spire.

He wondered if the missile could pick up information through visual sensors implanted in its hull, and what the brain might think of Phoenix which, from his height, must be like an open book spread out for all to read.

Jack, for one, couldn't read this age. The memories of other lives interfered with his understanding. The new America constantly amazed him. The streets of Phoenix, for example, wound themselves around and around a center like lines on a conch shell, narrow and crowded. The simplicity of the constructions didn't explain the pattern. All the houses had a fundamental similarity, as if the primitive builders were informed by an invisible Spirt and labored like ants to construct Its hidden forms. All over America, in endless variations, he had observed the same phenomenon, the birth of a new form world, still tentative, groping, and unsure of itself, but recognizably the same.

He shook his head and felt regret that he hadn't studied history in any of his lives. With more information, he might understand why this America reminded him of hives. Oval shapes dominated the architecture. The buildings seemed to hang between upright columns, giant pods, modified only at the base where the requirements of physics overcame the cultural tendency. Inside the houses—they reached several storeys into the vertical—spiralling stairs led from level to level and corridors criss-crossed each level in that random pattern which everyone born into this century (without memories of other times) found perfectly sensible.

Community, communality, he thought, and it occurred to him that mankind might be planning a new adaptation of which the architecture was but an outward sign: a style and a feeling which might prevent, once Science awoke again, the creation of such monstrosities as that thing above, a brass bell that had no charity. As yet Jack saw no other sign of such a desirable adaptation, but the buildings, cities, and many forms of family organization predicted it as through a glass, darkly.

He waited a while longer and let the darkness settle in. When it came, it was nearly total. Without electricity, these new cities died with sunset. Glass was a rarity, the climate unreasonably cold, and people shut their windows tight with heavy wooden shutters insulated with bits of cloth at the cracks. Only a few people moved about in the light of torches.

At last, feeling that it was safe enough, Jack moved toward the tower—it was little more than a framework, really, and he slipped between its heavy supports seeking a ladder. He found it soon, a rough, makeshift affair built for workmen. He took a breath and began the long ascent.

Standing on a narrow platform and surprised somewhat that wind gusted up here while below it had been calm, Jack approached the missile. It hung in a network of leather straps. He rapped his knuckles against the metal of its hull. The act evoked a dull sound.

Jack wondered if he would achieve what he planned. He hoped he would. Otherwise his life might be snuffed out, along with hers, and their reunion might have to wait another growing up.

"Hi there," Jack said.

"What? Who's there?"

The voice sounded sleepy, but Jack knew this to be illusion. Neuro-fibers linked the brain to a computer. The computer spliced together phrases from a tape-bank—pre-recorded phrases spoken by a pleasant baritone, an actor's rich warble.

"John Clark, at your service," Jack said. In the presence of this thing, his old American name came more naturally than 'Tankers Jack.' "I came to ask after your health. Are you operational? Or did you get damaged in the war? Your hull seems battered a good deal. Your rocket thrusters are gone. I'm surprised you're still alive."

The missile gleamed in silence, in a state of shock. Then the pleasant baritone spoke quickly. The voice had no emotional toning, but Jack sensed nevertheless a wild excitement beneath the words.

"Jesus Christ," the baritone said. The voice trembled from the center of the needle, a darkish reticulation in the metal. "Don't tell me you understand me? John Clark, did you say? What is this? What year is this? Oh, never mind. I am hallucinating. Stop your tricks, Frankie. Just stop it; don't torture me. Hello? Are you still there? Is anybody out there?"

"I'm here," Jack said. "John Clark, recently with the AEC."

"AEC?" Oh, Jesus! Frankie, for God's sake, why don't you just let me sleep in peace. These dreams!"

"I take it that your visual sensors are out of order?"

"Visual sensors! *Visual sensors*, the guy says. I'll be damned. You've just got to believe! You better believe they're out of order. I'm as blind as a bat. Blind, impotent, immobile, and crazy. That's me. Frank J. Harmon, at your service. CR 17459110."

"What does 'CR' stand for?"

"You don't know? Hell's bells, the guy might be for real. Not an illusion. 'Conscious Rocket,' John Clark. That's your name, isn't it? Clark?"

"John Clark, Mr. Harmon."

"Mister. He knows how to say *mister*. Glor by!"

"I am a skilled nuclear engineer, Mr. Harmon, lately with the AEC, like I said. Now retired. I thought I might help you, if I *can* help you. The natives around here tell me that you're unhappy."

The missile was silent again. A faint new moon had risen over the horizon. It was just a blur of light in the perpetual murk of the atmosphere but bright enough to ease forth a shadowy outline of the city below.

The missile suddenly burst out: "Unhappy, did you say? I'll give you unhappy, Mr. Clark. How would you like to live the life I've lived. Quadruple amputee? Get it? If you're with the AEC, you'll remember that war. We called it the Palestine Insertion Operation. A great big dong slipped right into Israel's see you, auntie. You get the picture. It got me then. Observers, we were called. But I am boring you! Tell me you're still there, John Clark."

"I'm here. I read you loud and clear, Frankie."

"Say it again."

"Say what again?"

"Say 'Frankie' again."

"Sure, Frankie. Any time."

"Man, that feels good. I get a real high, hearing that word. Jesus Christ!"

"You were telling me your story, Frankie."

"Johnny, bless you, how I groove on you. My story? What a trip. Real fun, being a basket case. Hester, my wife. She met me at the airport when they brought us back, and she had a look in her eyes, let me tell you. You don't know that look, how could you? I don't know the look myself, any more. I've been in this darkness all this time. What do I know about seeing any more. I just see this darkness, and I hear all sorts of things. I am a real good listener now. Never was a listener before. But I listened real hard to Hester. Night and day. I heard her on the telephone whispering to the Veterans Administration by the hour. And her whispering to little Tom—Tom's my son, you see—telling him Daddy's very, very sick. And then they had this hush-hush program to find astronauts. Physical impairments were said to be no impediment, in fact preferred. Am I losing you, Johnny? Are you still there? I don't know how to tell a story any more."

"I am with you, Frankie. They wanted you to be an astronaut."

"Yes, sir. Useful again. Learn new skills. Earn a lot of money for Hester. Little Tommy could wear a button in the school: My Daddy is an Astronaut. Red white and blue. Say it again, Mr. Clark."

"Frankie," Jack said.

"Thanks. Thanks a lot. I needed that. So I signed an agreement. Hester said it was all right. I had trouble reading. Even then, something with my eyes. They promised to fix that, in astronaut school. I held the ballpoint between my teeth. They had a guy from NASA there. He was a notary. He signed a certificate to prove that my scrawl was really mine. It looked like some kid's doodle. Didn't look like Frank J. Harmon at all. Never would have made it as a painter. Making watercolors for Christmas cards. You know what that is? Christmas cards? Johnny!"

"I am present and accounted for, Frankie.

Christmas cards were sent at Christmas to all those dear and near. Okay? We cared enough to send the very best."

"Bless you, Johnny. Hallmark Cards. Oh, bless you, bless you, bless you. Can you help me? Help me, Johnny. I want to see again."

"I'll do my best, Frank, old buddy. But tell me what happened? Did they kill you and put you in a machine?"

" 'Death takes place when cerebral functions cease,' " Frankie quoted. "They didn't kill me. No sirree. I signed that authorization, didn't I? It said that I agreed to accept prosthetic devices that would restore my useful functioning. Didn't I? You tell me. I did. It looked like a kid's doodle, but it was done by yours truly, a ballpoint between the teeth, eyes crossed, almost, to try to see the paper. The small print was blurred. Get the picture, Johnny? Johnny?"

"Frankie."

"You're for real, aren't you?"

"I'm for real," Jack said.

"Mind you, Johnny, I didn't kick. (Not that I had anything to kick with.) Forst off they put these probes into my brain, and next thing you know, I was having sex. Wild, unbelievable. Better than ever with Hester or anyone else. Wow! They just tickled something in the brain, and there I was, flipping out. Kama Sutra, baby. Real unbelievable, like. They did it when we were cooperative, and you've never seen a bunch of studs cooperate like we did. It went on and on, even after we were implanted in the ships. I remember standing there, on my launching platform, eyes out over the Pacific, this giant thing all around me, and my brain feeling the hydraulic fluids gush and swish about, and I'd be having these orgasms up there, one after the other, Jesus Christ, Johnny! Johnny?"

"Frankie, would it help if I put my hand on your hull? Can you feel it?"

"No. All gone. Sensory's gone, visual's gone, mobile is gone, sex is gone. There's nothing but these thoughts and dreams and hallucinations. Say, how long was I out there, in the swamp?"

"Were you in a swamp?"

"You didn't know that? In a swamp. The sunlight barely reached down. I almost died. Even now, it's weaker than it used to be. Or else my memory is failing. I got lost, coming back, after the great Telepathic Conference we held, we and the Chinese missiles, above the Pacific. We could talk to each other without the voice tapes. No language barrier, either. They sent me back, headed for Houston. Something went wrong on the way. My eyes, I think. Never any good to start with. Hell of a thing. Here I'd been an observer, you know, watching that famous insertion. And next thing you know, some little wire must have burned up. Look ma. No arms, no legs, no eyes. And no sex, either. They controlled that from someplace central. Dole you out an orgasm every now and then. Obedience earned it for you. Good boys get to do whoopee. But something got Central early in the war. Get the picture? Johnny?"

"Here I am," Jack said and pounded on the hull. "You feel that?"

"Faintly, old friend. I hear the vibrations. I can't feel anything on the outside. Feeling's all gone."

"What about inside," Jack asked. "Your explo-

sive charge—is that in good shape? Could you
. . . still explode?"

"Don't be shy," Frankie said. "I know I'm a
bomb. We found that out after a while. Telepathy,
you know. We could feel our buddies dying. Odd
sensation, filled with sex desire. You believe in
reincarnation?"

"Sometimes, Frankie."

"Well, I do," the missile said. "I've been trying
to get myself killed. Now I'm not so sure. A guy
has to have a friend. Are you there, friend?"

"I'm here, right next to you," Jack soothed. "I
asked about your insides."

"You sure did, Johnny, and I don't mind telling
you. I think it's still all there. I check every now
and then. Guy in my condition, he's got to know
about his death. You know what I mean? That's all
I've got going for me. I need a good impact on the
nose of this thing. Set off the electrical impulse to
start the fusion, drive the mass together. Critical
mass. Hey, man. The last big orgasm."

"Did you talk these people into dropping you?"

"Did I? I tried. But I'm blind as a bat. They
thought I was God, and I sort of went along. Told
them to drop me and I'd come out. Savage types,
would you say? Like those Palestinians I helped
insert. But don't tell the press. You're not press,
are you?"

"No. I'm just a retired guy, AEC, like I said."

"Good. Don't tell them we helped with the
fighting. Not supposed to do that. Observers just
observe. Get it?"

"I get it."

"Oil shortage still critical? Is there still a shortage?"

"Not that I can tell," Jack said. He glanced about involuntarily. Phoenix lay there, a dark crowding of oddly arranged pods. The streets wound around and around in a spiralling coil toward the nub of the city, lines on a conch shell, and this square the center of the world.

"You don't really want to die," Jack said.

"I don't? Maybe I don't. But it sure is boring in here. You can't believe what it was like, in the swamp. It gurgled the whole time. I must have been down there more than a year."

"Would you believe a century?"

"What?!"

"Two and a half centuries?"

"Jesus. But . . . but then how come you know the things you know? Is there still an AEC? All these savages?"

"Don't fret about that," Jack said. "Can you open your hull? I'd like to look inside you, look at your charge. Can you give me access?"

Frankie hesitated. The wind was gusting.

"You're my friend, aren't you?"

"I'm your friend, Frankie. Here's what I'll do for you. I'll fix your eyes again—if they can be fixed. And I'll keep you company. Who knows, I might even find a way to give you sex again. But you've got to help me. You're hanging in a tower in the middle of a city. If they drop you, you'll get what you want. You'll die and go to paradise. But so will all the people around here—and for miles around. You don't want that kind of orgasm, do you?"

"Wait a minute!" Frankie said. The baritone had no emotional toning, but Jack sensed challenge in the words.

"Just a little minute, friend. Do you think I care? You think I give a damn? Haven't I done my share? Who are these people, anyway? I can't see a soul. What gives you the right to tell me how to die. I get it. You're trying to trick me. AEC, did you say? Well, let me tell you something, buddy. You guys were always jealous of us NASA types. No spa, old friend. Are you there? Johnny?"

Jack stood on the platform and didn't say a word.

"Johnny? For crying out loud, say something."

Jack said nothing.

"Johnny, please. No offense. Look. I'm opening the panel for you. See, I'm your friend. I trust you. Say something."

"I'm watching, Frankie," Jack said. He observed a straight crack in the silvery hull. It grew larger as a piece of the metal slid smoothly away to the inside. He stepped closer and looked in. "It's too dark to see inside," he said.

"I'll make you a light." A glow illuminated masses of componentry.

"Explain what I am looking at," Jack said.

"The charge is that flat octagon on the right," Frankie explained. "Or maybe, from your perspective, it's on the left. I don't know my spatial arrangements. The gyro is shot. See it? Johnny?"

"I see it, Frank."

"All right, buddy. Now, on the left, or maybe on the right—"

"Frankie, that tiny little thing? That's the charge?"

"Charge? Did I say charge? I meant the trigger. It's a fusion trigger. It's small, all right. Progress,

you know. Just a bunch of mirrors and a vacuum.
Stop that. It feels like a tickle."

"It's welded in there," Jack said. "How can I get
it out."

"It just looks like a weld, old friend. Electrosta-
tic adhesion. I can snap it loose for you—if I want
to."

"Snap it, then."

"I'll snap it when I know I can trust you. Can I
trust you, Johnny? Johnny? *Johnny!* . . . Sure, I
can trust you, there, see? I snapped it loose for
you. Now you've got it, Johnny. You've got my
manhood. I gave you everything I've got. My
death is all I've got to give. Get it? Johnny, I love
you, see? I love you. Hey, Johnny!"

"I'm here, Frank. I'm looking at this thing. What
would happen if they dropped you now? Any
chance for a big bang?"

"No way," Frankie said. "Like I told you. I gave
you my manhood. Without that trigger, no critical
mass. Need that fusion to melt the walls to suck
the hot stuff into the center by the inertial. Figured that out, in the swamp. All dispersed now,
between my parts, the stuff. Iridium walls. Safe as
anything. Johnny?"

"I'm here, Frankie. I'm with you. Now listen.
It's night time right now, and I need light to work
on you. You got to sleep now, and tomorrow we'll
talk again. I'll work on your eyes, first thing.
Okay?"

"Don't leave me," said the mellow baritone,
without emotional toning. But underneath Jack
sensed a growing anguish.

IX

ALANS SHEPHERD strode down the corridor in the
wake of the soldier who had come to get him.
Anger boiled inside his head and guts. The
messenger had interrupted his dinner preparations. Shepherd seldom made such preparations, but this time was unique.

Zeronica had sent him an invitation to attend
the celebration banquet. A written invitation. His
secretary, a Dingbat named Birdie, had read it out
to him in her ancient cackle. Then Birdie had
smiled slyly.

But Shepherd had fewer hopes than the feathery fem. Zeronica couldn't be trusted. Nevertheless, the invitation kindled hopes he had seen
turn to ash. But Godbod only knew! Perhaps she
had changed her mind and would fulfill him,
now, at last. The matter with the needle had
worked out after all. And the other day, looking
up at the tower his men had built in record time,
Zeronica had praised his skill in words of startl-

ing kindness. Tomorrow the world would see 'epiphany.' Birdie had told him what the word meant: God's appearance among men. The voice inside the needle would show itself in fire and lightning, thunder and smoke. Phoenix would become a shrine, the magnet of a grand, yearly pilgrimage.

Now it was moments before the bell would call the banquet. The interruption came at a terrible time. A scribe, the soldier had said. What sort of scribe could convince the guard to violate orders. No business. Not tonight. Some scribe. Terribly persuasive fellow. Well, he would be persuading rats tonight. In the dungeon. Insolent creature.

Moments later Shepherd sat down behind a table and they showed the scribe in, closed the door. He was dark, slender, and had long, sensitive fingers. Moist eyes looked at Shepherd from beneath the shadow of a black hat's rim. A golden earring dangled from his ear and reflected the shine of torches stuck into wrought iron holders in the wall.

Shepherd felt a rippling shudder pass down his back, an unpleasant sensation of tingling cold. The eyes across the table infused him with fear; so did the hint of a smile around those sensuous lips. His own steady face stiffened. He laid his hands on the table and stared at the scribe.

"What can I do for you," he said, using words much milder than he had intended.

The scribe sat down without an invitation.

"I am told I must get your permission to see your mistress, the president-person."

"That may be," Shepherd responded. "*If* you get to see her. Which isn't sure at all."

"I expect to see her. Immediately," the scribe said, smiling.

"What makes you think that?" Shepherd challenged. So doing, he felt uncertainty in his stomach. The scribe sent out vibrations. They cramped Shepherd's innards.

"I have information of the greatest urgency."

"Then tell me."

"I'll tell the president-person and no one else."

"In that case you might die with your news," Shepherd said coolly. He hoped the scribe had heard the threat.

"I don't think so," the scribe said. "Does the name Theodore Aspic mean anything to you?"

Shepherd shook his head. He felt the chill again. It ran down his back. Someone had walked across his grave, or some such nonsense.

"Did you know that the ritual machinery installed in the upper portion of Plutonium has been destroyed?"

"What ritual machinery?" Shepherd asked. He wondered what in the world the man wanted and why he felt so nauseous. Could this scribe be a magician? "Try to make sense, man. I'm busy. I can't fool around with you all night." He cocked his head, listening for the bell.

"Then take me to your mistress," said the scribe.

"So far you haven't given me a good enough reason."

"Does the name John Clark ring a bell?"

Shepherd shuddered. The man across the table had an uncanny look. He seemed familiar in some way. Was he someone Shepherd had met in his bandit days? Was he someone Shepherd had *killed!* The thought gave him another cold shiver. He didn't believe in ghosts. No way.

"I have vital information about the brain-missile," the scribe said.

"The *what*?"

"The bomb."

"What bomb?"

"The bomb you've got hanging in the tower. The talking bomb."

"Godbod?"

"Godbod, if you like."

The scribe reached into a satchel he carried at his side. He took from it an odd-looking something. An Old Order mystery. He laid it on the table. It was flat and had eight points. Reddish eyes seemed to be arranged on its surface.

"What is that?"

"It's a fusion trigger. You should know. You were a physicist once."

Shepherd stared at the scribe. The man appeared to be sane, but his words were troubled and incomprehensible.

"I took it out of . . . Godbod tonight. I went up there and had a chat with it."

"You're insane," Shepherd cried. "FRANKLIN!" he yelled. A soldier looked in through the door. "Take this character and lock him up."

"Just a minute," the scribe said calmly. He showed no fear or excitement. "Your mistress will want to know why Godbod gave me this precious part of himself. Don't you think? What if nothing happens tomorrow when your people cut the straps and the thing falls down. Wouldn't you want to know? How will you explain that?"

"Get out of here, Franklin," Shepherd shouted at the soldier. Darkness surrounded him. He didn't know what he was doing. The door closed.

"Look," he said, pointing a finger at the scribe. "If this is a trick, I'll personally see to it that. . . ." His finger wobbled threateningly.

"No trick," the scribe said.

Shepherd stared at him. In the silence between them, nausea groped toward his stomach.

"Five minutes," he said. "You'll have five minutes with her. No more. And you better make sense."

He rose. Hollowly, through the intricately arranged walls of the presidential pod, he heard the chime calling the banquet.

"Five minutes," he repeated, and he pointed to a sand-clock on the corner of the desk.

He watched while the scribe put away the mystery. Then he left the room. The scribe followed him. Shepherd looked over his shoulder. "And what do they call you?"

"Tankers Jack," the scribe said.

Shepherd turned the name this way and that. It had no echoes, meant nothing at all, had no effect. He had never heard of a Tankers Jack, nor of a Tanker. The man was not some enemy's son, no matter how familiar he looked. But he was persuasive, dammit. And oddly frightening. His eyes ruled Shepherd's, much as Zeronica's did. Shepherd, though aware of this wouldn't let the knowledge surface.

The presidential pod was a multi-structure. They had to pass from the eastern to the central portion of it by way of a covered bridge. In its middle Tankers Jack suddenly stopped, his hand on Shepherd's sleeve. His right hand described the panorama of rooftops with a wave.

"Fancy meeting like this again," he said. "In such a setting."

"I've nver laid eyes on you before," Shephered said with fright. He jerked his arm out of the scribe's hand. Phoenix lay before them. The tower loomed immediately up ahead, a wooden structure so skillfully erected and in such record time. Shepherd glanced up and saw Godbod's dull shimmer up there, half hidden by sections of timber. The moon, having risen high, enhanced its silvery glow.

"Your memory fails you, Alans Shepherd," the scribe said. "But never mind that. I wonder if your mistress will remember me."

Shepherd shuddered. He walked on, trying to shake off the eerie feeling. Deep down he experienced a tiny despair, a dark kind of knowing. It came into his being through chinks in the armour of his moral darkness. He stood before some kind of test, but didn't know it. To him it was simply a wrench of nausea.

They entered the banqueting chamber some moments later. The guests had not yet settled down. Zeronica throned in a sitting-basket hung from the ceiling by a chain. Senators and congressmen stood about her drinking beer from mugs. Her posture was regal. Her hands rested on the basket's arms, her gaze was steady. One of her legs was pulled up on the silken cushion.

Shepherd approached over the burned tile floor. His spurs rang like bells. Suddenly the scribe broke from his side and, with quickened strides, went ahead. Shepherd saw him bow before Zeronica. He did so in a strange way. His hat swept the floor in an exaggerated gesture. One of his legs was pulled back, the other stuck forward.

"Zeronica," the scribe said. His voice was melodious and rang through the hall. "I have sought you for centuries, my lady. It is a pleasure to see you so well—and so beautiful."

Congressmen and senators, ladies-in-wait, and even the beeman servants preparing the tables to the right, the small one and the large one, looked up and stared with surprise at this common, shabby figure, dressed like a vagabond.

Shepherd made haste to reach Zeronica's side. "Mistress," he began, "I apologize for this . . ."

She silenced him with a wave of her hand. Her eyes were fixed on the dark face of the scribe. Fear stabbed Shepherd as he watched her. Something in her features had softened, perhaps in response to the scribe's small smile.

"Step closer," she said to the man. "I take it you're not from these parts. Did I meet you on my tour?"

"You met me on your tour," the scribe affirmed. "Don't I look familiar?"

Zeronica hesitated, a finger in front of her lips. "Y-yes," she said. "Something about you does seem . . . But, frankly, I don't recall our meeting."

"That may be so," the scribe came back. He tossed his head and made the earring glimmer. Then he looked down. "I am an inconsequential scribe, my lady. If I were to suggest to you that we were close friends once, it would be presumption on my part, however true it may be." He looked up. "I sought you out, lady, drawn by my memories of you—and also because I heard of your interest in Old Order mysteries. Over the years, I have become a master—"

"Mistress," Shepherd broke in harshly, "this scribe came to me and demanded—"

"Shush," Zeronica said, her eyes on the scribe. "A master of the mysteries?" she asked.

"If I may be so bold," the scribe said.

"In that case," Zeronica said, "perhaps you would care to take dinner with me?"

"Your suggestion is my deepest wish," the scribe said, bowing.

Darkness closed in over Shepherd as dinner advanced. Until this day he had hoped, however small the hope, that Zeronica would someday be his. She had shown little interest in him. But she had scorned other men as well—which had reassured him. But what he saw tonight made his heart heavy. Waves came together over his head.

Upon his entrance into the room, Shepherd had noticed the small table, some distance from the large one, with two couches positioned side-by-side along its low, triangular surface. Despite the scribe's disturbing presence, he had spied that table, off to the side, and a thrill had passed through his bowels, despite the nausea. He had divined, in a flash, that she had meant to dine with him. Alone. With him, with Alans Shepherd, the guest of honor at this banquet celebrating epiphany. He had brought the God-bod. He deserved her special favor.

But now, cruelly, she lay on one couch and *he* lay on the other. He, the scribe. The creature called Tankers Jack. As for Shepherd—whistling beemen had brought an extra couch for him. They had placed it at the big table. Where the senators and congressman reclined between chattering ladies-in-wait.

Zeronica behaved oddly, and the talk at Shepherd's table turned around that subject. The high-placed guests threw Shepherd furtive glances as they gossiped. They knew the couch had been meant for him. Now they saw Zeronica giggle in an uncontrolled way. Then again her eyes were fixed on the scribe's dark features as he spoke. Only his golden ring seemed to move. He mesmerized her. She forgot to eat. But then, thinking he had bound her long enough, the scribe made lively gestures and jokes. Then she laughed again and reached for morsels of food on her plate. The sequence repeated and went on and on.

As hours passed, the company grew restless. Dentons Howard fell asleep on his couch, a fat senator. A lady-in-wait shook him from time to time to stop his raspy snores. Others drank gloomily and wondered when she might announce the end. Her banquet speech had not been delivered. She seemed to have forgotten the occasion. Instead her shiny blondness moved closer and closer to that dark head adorned by moist eyes and sensuous lips. One or two torches went out and smoked black against the wall. Only the chief beeman stayed around. He sat on a chair inside the door that led to the kitchen. His bony legs were visible; the rest of him leaned back, out of sight. He probably dozed.

Shepherd couldn't stand another minute of it. He rose abruptly. He left without the customary farewells to the hostess. His spurs rang angrily on tile. He wheeled about at the door, but Zeronica hadn't even turned her head.

He meant to go back to his quarters. His few belongings would be quickly packed. He would call the men whom he controlled, his orignal band, and before dawn's rust rose above the horizon, he would leave Phoenix, shaking dust from his boots. But halfway down the corridor that led to the bridge that led to east pod where his own quarters lay. Shepherd stopped and turned around. Curiosity ate him like acid. His eyes hungered to see the end. A gorgeous fury assailed him. On the way back, without thinking, he took a curved sword from a wall rack and slipped it inside his tunic. Then, stealthily, he inserted himself into a children's corridor.

By the time he found a spot where the wall, broken by wooden trellis work, gave him a view of the banquet hall, most of the guests had taken leave. They had followed Shepherd's example. Only Dentons Howard snored loudly, without inhibitions, on the couch. The chief of the beemen cleared the table. Then he also took his leave.

Shepherd watched, his breath a hot reflection from the trellis. They rose at last and walked away, hand in hand. Shepherd followed them using children's corridors. His boots, left behind, couldn't reveal his movements. His naked feet stirred the dust of these unused pathways.

He lay on his stomach one floor above, eyes before another trellis. He tried to pierce the darkness. But he could see nothing below. Only his ears told him that they made love beneath him on the presidential bed. He began to sob without sound.

Later he listened to silence, then to whisperings. The curved blade pressed against his body beneath the tunic, but he didn't have the heart to pull it out, to plunge into the dark room where they breathed, to avenge Zeronica's treachery once and for all. Something paralyzed his hands and will. A little gap in his moral darkness allowed light to shine through. The light came from her and also, oddly, from him. When, after a while, they began again and he heard her soft moaning like a fist in his gut, Shepherd rose and retraced his steps, his desolation hardening to ice. Yes, ice. Go home, bandit. Go home. His sobs subsided and his eyes dried out. He put on his boots again and went away across the bridge. His feet tinkled like bells.

He decided that he couldn't harm her. But neither would he let her keep the gift that he had brought her, the ultimate gift, the last thing that she had said she needed to put Phoenix in the center of the world.

Grim of face, he roused his men and whispered orders. They sat up in their beds and rubbed their eyes. Then, groggily, they got up and groped for clothing.

Jack woke suddenly. He had been dozing. Zeronica's arm lay across his chest, and her shallow breath moved against his shoulder. He felt anguish, although he didn't know its source. It seemed that a voice had exploded in his head. A baritone had called for Johnny. Dreaming of the missile? He listened but heard nothing out of the ordinary. She slept beside him. Somewhere a cricket chirped. Nevertheless, Jack thought he heard the echoes of dying sound.

He began to move but gave it up. Blissful peace bathed his senses. He was at home, at last. She was his now, as she had been meant to be. Their lives, separated by his karmic fall, had entwined again. He knew now how to win her favor, the Cosmic Flower's soft embrace. Kindness would do it. Love of man and beast. Love, even of brains encased in steel and wire.

He heard a noise and stiffened. There was no help for it. He had to rise.

He disentangled himself carefully, unwilling to wake her. The room was chilly and the tile floor downright cold. He was groping toward the wall, expecting a window in that direction, when he heard shouts and the drum of horses' hoofs on cobble-stone. He ran the rest of the way, found the window, and threw open the heavy shutters.

The window opened on Phoenix Square. Moonlight bathed the scene. He saw motion to his right. Horses disappeared into one of his coiling streets, two lines of horses stretching some kind of netting between them. Something gleamed like silver between the lines. Then they were gone.

Jack looked up into the tower, filled with sudden insight. Frank J. Harmon, brain-missile, Godbod, had disappeared.

Jack swallowed. He knew, suddenly, that he had lost a friend.

EPILOGUE

It never came to a military clash between Phoenix and Plutonium. A delegation of the Hierarchy went through the city sniffing for the needle while the monkish thousands sat in siege outside the city walls. Satisfied, at last, Plutonium believed a man called Tankers Jack who had done the negotiating. They went away to trail one Alans Shepherd, plutonium thief.

Many years later word filtered back of a great new cult that had been started high up north, where the ice begins. The place attracted many pilgrims who went there to consult the oracle. Godbod had appeared to men, the rumors said. You asked it a question and it sometimes answered and sometimes it said nothing. But you paid for your chance anyway and you had one turn of the sand-clock to make a go of it. When blind men came, the oracle always spoke, and many blind men settled in the region and sold their services. The guardians of Godbod grew powerful and rich. They built a great temple and called it Harmony. People said that it was gold and silver, inside and out, and that its bells were heard for many kemits, round about, echoing over the ice.

The president-person of Phoenix married the scribe called Tankers Jack. She made him chief of her special priesthood, and they worked behind a high fence with all manner of mysteries. In a ceremony in Phoenix Square, right in front of the presidential pod, Zeronica changed her name again. She named herself Monica. She sent out runners to advertise the fact. They explained the meaning of her name so even dullards would get the picture.

They lived happily ever after, she and he. And after . . . and after . . . and after . . . like figures between double mirrors, getting ever smaller in a stream of time.

Ursula K. Le Guin

10705	**City of Illusion**	$2.25
47806	**Left Hand of Darkness**	$2.25
66956	**Planet of Exile**	$1.95
73294	**Rocannon's World**	$1.95

Available wherever paperbacks are sold or use this coupon

POUL ANDERSON

78657	**A Stone in Heaven**	$2.50
20724	**Ensign Flandry**	$1.95
48923	**The Long Way Home**	$1.95
51904	**The Man Who Counts**	$1.95
57451	**The Night Face**	$1.95
65954	**The Peregrine**	$1.95
91706	**World Without Stars**	$1.50

Available wherever paperbacks are sold or use this coupon

ACE SCIENCE FICTION WAREHOUSE
P.O. Box 400, Kirkwood, N.Y. 13795

Please send me the titles checked above. I enclose _____.
Include 75¢ for postage and handling if one book is ordered; 50¢ per
book for two to five. If six or more are ordered, postage is free. California, Illinois, New York and Tennessee residents please add sales tax.

NAME_____

ADDRESS_____

CITY_____STATE_____ZIP_____

Ace Trade Publications

Gordon R. Dickson	**LOST DORSAI**	$4.95
Dean Ing	**SOFT TARGETS**	$4.95
Larry Niven	**THE MAGIC GOES AWAY** (Illustrated)	$4.95
	THE PATCHWORK GIRL (Illustrated)	$5.95
Jerry Pournelle	**A STEP FARTHER OUT** (Science Fact)	$6.95
Fred Saberhagen	**THE EMPIRE OF THE EAST** (Fantasy)	$6.95
Lynn Abbey	**DAUGHTER OF THE BRIGHT MOON** (Fantasy)	$6.95
	THE BLACK FLAME (Fantasy)	$6.95
Robert W. Prehoda	**YOUR NEXT FIFTY YEARS** (Science Fact)	$5.95
Roger Zelazny	**THE CHANGELING** (Illustrated)	$7.95
Harry G. Stine	**THE SPACE ENTERPRISE** (Science Fact)	$6.95
Frederick Pohl	**SCIENCE FICTION: STUDIES IN FILM** (Illustrated)	$6.95

Available wherever paperbacks are sold or use this coupon

126b

FRITZ LEIBER

FAFHRD AND THE GRAY MOUSER SAGA

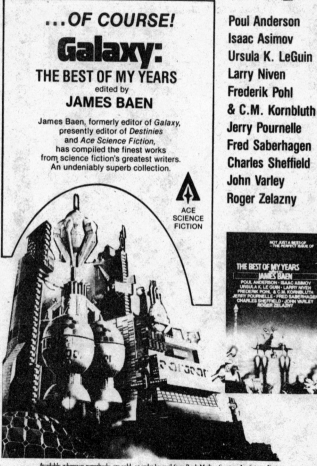